Nellie Bishop

CLARA GILLOW CLARK

BOYDS MILLS PRESS

Published by Caroline House
Boyds Mills Press, Inc.
A Highlights Company
815 Church Street
Honesdale, Pennsylvania 18431
Printed in the United States of America

Publisher Cataloging-in-Publication Data
Clark, Clara Gillow.
Nellie Bishop / by Clara Gillow Clark.—1st ed.
[200]p. : ill. ; cm.
Summary : Nellie struggles to survive in the rough and tumble world of a
Pennsylvania canal town.
ISBN 1-56397-491-6
1. Canals—Pennsylvania—Juvenile fiction. 2. Pennsylvania—History—1783-
1865—Juvenile fiction. [1. Canals—Pennsylvania—Fiction. 2. Pennsylvania—
History—1783-1865—fiction.] I. Title.
813.54—dc20   [F]   1996   AC
Library of Congress Catalog Card Number 95-76355

First edition, 1996
Book designed by Jean Krulis
The text of this book is set in 12.5 point Berkeley Book.

10 9 8 7 6 5 4 3 2

To my best friend, Frog
—From your loving Toad

Chapter 1

As dusk settled over the town, Nellie Bishop felt as if a dark veil had been drawn over her life. Only a few hours earlier that June day of 1886, Miss Sutton had pressed a *McGuffey Reader* into Nellie's hands and wished her a good life. "May Providence be with you," the teacher had said kindly.

It was Nellie's last day of common school; she was thirteen. She had known this day would come. But until now she had managed to thrust away the unsavory truth. As darkness approached, Ma had opened the old trunk with great ceremony and pulled out the costume—the one her older sisters had worn— the costume worn to catch a man.

Nellie stood stiff and mute as Ma dressed her. Ma mumbled to herself as she worked. "I'll soon have one less mouth to feed and coins in me hand. New stockings, new shoes. It's shameful for a washer-woman to go about like this. You'll change all that for me, won't you, dearie?"

Ma took quick puffs on her pipe as she pondered her sure-to-come wealth. But the truth, Nellie knew, was that Ma would get nothing new, that their debts in town would not be settled, and that any fresh coins would warm Pa's palm for gambling. The truth, Nellie knew, was that Ma would get cast-off garments from the uptown folk, the Irish grocer would have to extend them more credit, and Pa would lose the coins in a card game. Seemed as if he always did. What good would coins do any of them?

As if sensing her thoughts, Ma yanked Nellie's hair, twisted it into a long switch, and fastened it up with amber combs, arranging the bangs in tight curls across Nellie's forehead. Ma then painted Nellie's cheeks with rouge, colored her lips scarlet, and powdered her freckles. On her arms and ears Ma placed cheap rubber jewelry.

At last Ma stood back and drew deeply on her pipe while she eyed her daughter. Nellie was taller than most girls and freckled, with light brown hair and eyes the color of grass in early autumn. "Handsome enough. Not coquettish looking like my other girls, though." Ma puffed out a cloud of smoke. "Got that unsullied look some men crave," she said. "Wonder what a man will pay to wed you?"

Nellie stood silent, frowning, while her mind raced with thoughts—thoughts of escape, thoughts of rebellion, thoughts of freedom. If she were a boy like her little brother, Willie, Ma wouldn't be forcing her to do this. Well, Ma might be able to force her to dress up, force her to go to the dance—but Ma could not force her to be pleasing to a man.

"Wipe that scowl off your face," Ma said as her eyes narrowed, and she struck Nellie with a sudden, swift movement. Ma's hand stung Nellie's cheek like a leather strap. "Let go your fool stubbornness, girl. Why you have to be so strange? Your sisters, each and every one, was pleased when their time came. Now it's your time, and you're goin' to Liberty Dance Hall, and you're gonna dance, gonna act sweet, gonna get yourself a husband. You hear, girl?"

Liberty Dance Hall was the congregating place for the Irish of Shanty Hill in the town of Dyberry Forks. Ma was proud that she had married off her three other daughters through the dance hall and gotten paid for the privilege. Her girls didn't go for free.

In the cool of twilight, Nellie and Ma walked slowly down the path toward Liberty Hall. It was no great distance—nothing in town was far away. Nellie walked stiffly, unaccustomed to shoes. Ma prodded her along with a stick as if she were a balking mule refusing to pull a loaded boat on the canal. Nellie heard the jeers and the tittering of women, heard the other girls as they passed swiftly by on their way to the dance.

She dug her nails into the flesh of her palms. Let them laugh, she thought. Not one of them cared for book learning, not one of them had lasted through the last term of common school. "What good will it serve you, Nellie?" the other girls had chided. "Books won't warm you in winter." She had no answer for them then, and none now. She had desired learning the way they desired marriage. Schooling was what Nellie had wanted, and Ma had been willing to let her have it—until Nellie had grown up enough to be wed.

Chapter 2

Liberty Hall was a large wooden structure with high, open rafters and rough, unfinished walls. The gaslights were as murky as distant moons viewed through a dense fog of smoke and dust. Nellie held back, pushing herself into a shadowy corner, her arms folded over her chest, a scowl set on her face. Ma circulated around the perimeter of the noisy room. Nellie watched as Ma singled out the unattached men. The men had more wits than the lads, she said, enough wits to put aside a coin, and Ma charged even for a dance with her daughters.

Ma laid a hand on the arm of a burly man and nodded in the direction of the wall where Nellie was trying to remain unnoticed. The man had wild red hair tumbling around his shoulders. His arms were thick and as solid looking as stone hitching posts.

He slipped some coins into Ma's outstretched hand and strode toward Nellie. As he came closer, she pushed herself deeper between the studs of the wall. She could see a chipped tooth, another one broken and decayed, and the lean, hungry look in his hard blue eyes.

She scowled and hunched herself into a deformed shape.

"Callahan," the man said. He reached out a powerful hand and yanked Nellie out into the light and onto the dance floor. A player piano, mechanically driven and out of control, played its tinny tunes without pretense of a musician—but the dancers didn't seem to notice. They whirled in the reels of dance, their faces lit with pleasure. As Callahan spun her, she caught sight of Ma's smug face, bright the way it always was when she had coins in her hand.

Nellie pulled away from the man's foul whiskey breath, but he snapped her back sharply and pinned her with an arm held tightly across her back. Then he propelled her beyond the circle of dancers, out of the gaslit hall, and into the darkness of the street.

"The woman said I could examine the goods," Callahan said, his hands starting to grope for her body.

Nellie pulled away. In the half-light of the street lamp she could see his eyes, blank and dumb. Almost without thinking, she rolled the saliva on her tongue and spat forcefully into his face.

Callahan roared angrily above the noise of the hall. Nellie fled into the darkness, kicking off the unfamiliar pumps; the amber combs flew out of her hair like sparks from a crackling fire. She would not have a canal man—a man like Pa, who was weak and strong in all the wrong ways. And this Callahan, she would not be his.

Chapter 3

Nellie and Willie were high up in the branches of an old maple. A sultry haze had settled over the town; not a breath of air stirred. A fortnight had passed since the last dance, and tonight there would be another at Liberty Hall. There would be men— maybe Callahan, with fresh wages ready to spend on whiskey and cards and dance. Nellie had seen the set of Ma's jaw earlier in the day and had slipped away while her mother was unsuspecting. No how was she going to get caught again.

"Nellie! Nellie Bishop!" Ma came out on the stoop and hollered, her hands cupped around her mouth.

As Ma's voice rasped out into the stagnant air, Nellie quickly pulled her bare feet up onto the limb out of sight. She winced as the sudden movement set her shoulders and back to throbbing. Her body still pained from the recent blows Ma had laid on her. She had run away from Callahan, she had lost the precious pumps and amber combs, and the unforgivable had occurred: Callahan had demanded that Ma give back his coins.

"Answer me, girl!" Ma hollered, her voice shrill.

But Nellie didn't. The sun was just slipping behind the church spires across the river; it was nearly dusk. Through the leaves, Nellie could see Ma angrily trying to peer into the brambles and tall weeds that grew on the hillside behind their broken down shanty.

"Listen to this, Nel," Willie said. He had a newspaper draped across his lap, a newspaper he'd swiped in town earlier that day. "'As Davey rode along, he spied a crowd gathering in front of the saloon. . . .'"

"Shush, Willie," Nellie whispered, giving him a dark look. "Ma might hear you!"

"Nellie Bishop, get down here, girl, or I'll wallop you good!"

"Can't wallop me if you can't find me," Nellie whispered. She knew that even if she did obey, Ma would still wallop her. There was just no pleasing Ma; she was cold and hard as a piece of anthracite. The only things that warmed her heart were rage, money, and occasionally, Willie.

"Can I finish reading this to you now?" Willie asked, rustling the paper.

Nellie held up a finger in caution. She peered out from an opening in the leaves again. Ma was disappearing through the doorway.

"Old witch!" Nellie sighed and leaned back against the tree trunk. "I hate her, Willie. Hate her to pieces," she said, wincing again as she rubbed a tender spot on her shoulder. "Why can't she let me be? All she's got on her mind is wedding me off to any man that will pay."

Willie just rolled his eyes and started reading from the western serial he was following in the *Herald*. "'Horses stood in the dusk. Low voices broke upon his ear. Davey was quick to sense the climate. He knew frontier towns in the cool of a summer evening when the calm was charged with trouble. And Davey sensed trouble tonight.'"

"It's trouble tonight if Ma catches me," Nellie said. "It's dreadful being a girl."

"Whoa!" Willie said. "Quit interrupting the story. What's ailing you, anyhow? Ma's gone. She won't corral you tonight," he said. "Here, Nel, this is what you need: 'Dr. Brady's Mandrake Bitters.' It cures 'bilious colic, bilious fever, dyspepsia, dropsy, diarrhea, depression of spirits . . .'"

"I don't need Dr. Brady's Bitters, Willie. I need Ma to stop painting me up, stuffing my front, decorating me with bangles and beads. I'm not going to any more dances at Liberty Hall just so she can hitch me up to some old canal rowdy like she did Rose and Blanche and Lizzie, and I'm not going to be examined like I was horseflesh for sale ever again."

Willie shook his head and grinned. "Well, Nellie, if you don't want to be a girl, and you don't aim to get hitched, what the heck do you want?"

Nellie frowned and swung her legs over the side of the limb. That was the problem—she didn't know. Inside her, something was stirring, a longing thick as cream, but a part of her knew that she might never find a tonic for what ailed her. If she were a man—like that Mr. Rockwell from uptown—she'd know the answer. At least she'd be free, wouldn't she? It was a sure thing that her pa wasn't free. Pa was bound to gambling the way a mule was bound to the loaded boats on the canal.

"I . . . I don't know, exactly," she said slowly as she climbed down. "I'm thinking. It'll come to me." But no matter how she focused on it, the feeling wouldn't take on a form she could name.

Willie folded up his newspaper and hid it in a hollow of the trunk. "You'd best make up your mind quick 'fore Ma gets you hitched."

Nellie was quiet for a moment. She wouldn't accept a foul man like that Callahan, but how could she escape Ma? "Come on," she said roughly, pushing away the ugly thoughts. "Let's get going."

Chapter 4

It was not yet dark when Nellie and Willie jumped down from the tree and followed the path they had made through the bushes, a safe path that led them away from Ma.

The path struggled through the rocks and scrub brush on the steep slope above the shanties and eventually wound its way to the river and the covered bridge at the lowest fringes of town. The Irish hill section was separated from the rest of the population by the Dyberry River. The river cut a long ribbon through the valley. On the thin side were the Irish poor, pushed up against the cliff wall on a meager strip of earth, their shacks dotting the craggy hillside.

But it was the Irish poor who had dug the canal that brought wealth to the town. The coal from the rich anthracite mines of the Moosic Mountains was shipped by rail to Dyberry Forks in northeastern Pennsylvania. A black mountain of anthracite, awaiting shipment by canal, could be seen from most anywhere in town. Down by the docks of the canal, the Irish still labored, shoveling coal and loading the boats for transport to supply the ever-hungry industries of New York City.

The remainder of the valley in which the small settlement had grown and thrived was also narrow. But still, Dyberry Forks had its share of impressive businesses and grand houses with expansive lawns, laid out on wide streets in uniform squares. At dusk, Nellie and Willie liked to prowl the streets of the prosperous uptown section.

Nellie loved this time of day. The town had gone quiet, with only the occasional clomp-clomping of a horse and buggy. Also, there was the lamplighter's magic as he trimmed and lit the gas lamps on the street corners, lighting the way before them like a firefly.

Willie always trailed behind her, his eyes trained on the dusty street, looking for a coin, a button, scraps of paper, nails lost from horseshoes. Willie didn't care—if it weren't dirt or horse droppings, chances are it'd end up in Willie's pocket. Willie always claimed he'd be a news reporter one day, but Nellie had her doubts. She feared Willie would end up working on the canal before long, just like all the other Shanty Hill boys. She shook her head. What could she do?

They walked through the covered bridge on the lower end of Dyberry Forks and made their way up Second Street, past the stench of the liveries, on by the National Hotel and Coyne House, and then past the quiet steepled churches that guarded the corners of Public Square. As they moved along in the shadows, the noise from downtown taverns—raucous voices, cursing, and slurred songs—spilled onto the side streets.

Occasionally, Willie would stop at a corner and watch a gang bunched together, shouting. Nellie would grab him and dart out of view, for Second Street ran parallel to the canal, with Front Street just one block away. She never allowed Willie to venture over to the canal section at night because it was inhabited mainly by rowdies and rats. It was not uncommon for either to be found dead in the murky waters of the canal basin.

Their destination was uptown, and as if affirming its own importance, uptown was separated from the canal and the commercial establishments by another change of course in the river's flow. The river valley became more generous in girth uptown. It was there that Willie found the best loot—and there that Nellie stole longing looks through the windows of seemingly happy homes.

Ma said that the uptown folk had it all. She'd seen it when she collected laundry at their back doors.

Ma said they had every contrivance known to man—electric lights, telephones, indoor privies.

The real ladies were seldom seen on downtown Front Street, but Nellie often watched them strolling in Public Square with their parasols and prams and fancy walking suits.

As soon as Nellie and Willie crossed over the uptown bridge, a self-conscious feeling came over Nellie. She sensed that it came over Willie, too, for he caught up to walk beside her. They both began to speak in whispers.

"Nel," he said urgently, nudging her arm. "I dare you—dare you to go up the lane to Homer Whyte's."

Nellie shook off his hand. Homer Whyte was just about the most famous man in the history of the town. He wrote books and poetry. His home was perched on a knoll above the grand houses of Dyberry Forks, and it was told on Shanty Hill that he kept mean dogs with powerful jaws. "No, Willie. How many times have I told you . . ." she said crossly.

"You never go where I want to," he said.

"Do too." Nellie kept on walking.

"No, you don't," Willie said, wetting his lips. "All I want to do is look."

"Well, I won't do it, 'cause you aim to do more than look. You aim to thieve, and we'd get caught. Do you want to get caught?"

"We won't."

"We won't 'cause I'm not going, and I'm not going to quarrel with you, Willie. I'm older, and I say we're not."

"Well, I say we are. You're not my boss. You'll never be, 'cause you're not a man."

Nellie whirled around and grabbed Willie by the shoulder. "Maybe I'm not a man, but that gives you no right . . . *no* right to push me around," she sputtered.

"Does too, and you know it," Willie said, pushing his face up close to hers.

Nellie shoved him away. "Then go by yourself, Willie." She turned and started walking, tears filling her eyes.

Willie trailed behind. He always did. But someday—maybe soon, Nellie thought—that would change. Change was coming; she felt it clean to the center of her heart. Willie was only ten, but lately he seemed to be taking on that roughness the older boys of the canal had. Still, he was small for his age, which was good. It would keep him in school longer than the other Shanty Hill boys. If only there was some way to keep Willie from going bad. . . .

Chapter 5

Nellie walked swiftly up North Front Street toward the Rockwell house. Willie scuffled along behind, muttering, "Just like Ma. That's what. Like Ma."

Nellie ignored him.

"Like Ma—a mean old witch." His voice grew louder. He strode up to walk beside her.

Anger swelled inside Nellie like a hot-air balloon. She was *not* like Ma! She curled her fingers into fists and pressed her lips tightly together. If Willie didn't hold his tongue, she'd be good and ready to punch him.

Willie went silent. He knew how to rile her good, but he also knew when to shush.

They moved off the street onto the sidewalk and continued along between the rows of maples and picket fences. Their steps slowed as they reached the iron fence surrounding the towering brick home of Mr. H. V. Rockwell. The house was built close to the street. Downstairs the windows were like doors—

hinged on one side and wide, with sills clear down to the porch floor. Tonight, the windows were opened out and the summer drapes pinned back. The great room was brilliantly lit; Nellie could see every last thing in detail, as if the sun had risen inside.

She and Willie crouched near a flowering rose-bush. Nellie pressed her face to the fence and inhaled the sweet fragrance. She reached through the bars, broke off a rosebud, and held it fast in her fingers. Surely no one would begrudge her so small a rose. Carefully she tucked it in her hair.

"Nel!" Willie said, grabbing her arm.

"Shh!" she hissed, shrugging off his hand. With the windows open, they'd have to be extra careful. Someone might hear them—or worse, see them. It would never do to be seen. She would feel so ashamed that she'd never risk coming here again.

Through the open windows, she could see the profile of Mr. Rockwell. He was sitting in an arm-chair near the window, reading. His wife sat facing him on a velvet settee, doing some sort of fancy needlework. But where were the daughters? The son? She wrapped her fingers tightly around the iron bars and waited. She heard the girls' laughter even before they came into the room.

"Oh!" She caught her breath as the two daughters stepped through the arched doorway, their heads close together, whispering and giggling the way they always did.

The father lay down his book when the girls came in. His voice boomed out. "My dears, you look lovely."

"Horatio!" the mother called out.

Horatio was the son, a little younger than Willie. He never seemed to stray far from his mother's side.

The girls, Jennie and Ellen, lifted their skirts and rushed to their father's side, their laughter tinkling out through the windows. "Papa! Papa!" They swooped down, planting kisses on the top of his head.

Nellie shivered and pressed closer to the bars. There was so much charity, so much pleasantness among them. Their affection seemed to come so easily, as easily as Ma's rages came to her.

Jennie curtsied before her father. "Papa," she said. But then her voice grew so soft that her words were lost to Nellie. Plainly the girls were showing off new costumes—Jennie in a cream brocade and Ellen in pink.

The little group seemed so close to her that Nellie longed to reach through the bars and touch the fabric of their gowns, capture some of their radiance for herself.

"Horatio?" the mother called again.

Horatio skulked in then, wearing knee britches,

his face puckered up in a sour pout about something. He pulled his wooden train set from a cupboard and flopped down on the polished floor near his mother.

Jennie walked over to the piano in the corner of the room and sat down. Her sister joined her.

Willie grabbed the bars with both hands. "I'm itching to lay hands on that train," he said.

"Shush now," Nellie said gently.

Then Jennie began to play. Nellie leaned against the fence and moved ever so slightly to the strains of the song. Her eyes closed. Oh, she imagined herself at such a grand piano, her fingers rippling over the keys. She knew every note by heart—it was "Moonlight Sonata." Miss Sutton, her old schoolteacher, would call her covetous and rap her knuckles with a cane if she could see her now. Yet it was the teacher who had encouraged her, taught her to read musical notes. Even Miss Sutton had been astounded when Nellie had played this very piece on the battered school piano.

Nellie opened her eyes and stared at the beautiful girl. Someday Nellie would play again. But this might be as close as she'd get to a real piano for a good long time.

"Pssst . . . Nel!" Willie called softly from somewhere in the darkness. She hadn't even noticed his absence. "Over here!"

Her heart began to thud loudly. Willie had climbed the fence. He was inside the yard! She tried to speak, but the words stuck in her throat.

"Catch!"

Something whizzed over her head in the darkness.

Nellie whirled around in time to see a ball drop to the ground and roll out into the street.

"Get it, Nel. Hurry!" Willie cried.

Not stopping to think, she shot out into the street.

"Whoa! WHOA!" a voice shouted. A horse whinnied loudly and reared up, one hoof nearly grazing her shoulder.

She froze. A moment later, someone grabbed her arm. A man towered over her.

Chapter 6

"What's going on out there?"

Nellie glanced back at the big house. Mr. Rockwell had stepped through the window and was peering into the darkness. Horatio jumped up and ran to join him, pointing and calling out.

Nellie's face burned with shame. There was no escape; she was held fast by their stares and by the grip of the strange man beside her. She lowered her head and stared at her bare feet.

"No need for alarm, folks!" called out the man with the horse.

Mr. Rockwell stood watching for a moment, then turned to go back inside with Horatio.

Where was Willie? Nellie wondered. Had he gotten back over the fence?

"You aren't hurt?" The man's voice sounded genuinely concerned.

"No," she said, looking away.

His hand grasped her arm more tightly now. "You

could have been killed! I almost ran over you. What are you doing here?"

Nellie tried to pull free. What was he going to do to her? It was plain enough that she didn't belong among these fine folks. With her free hand she smoothed the wrinkles of her faded gingham and wet her lips. She shook her head without answering. What could she say—"Oh, my brother was stealing and I was helping him. . ."?

He dropped her arm. "It's dangerous for a young girl to be out at night in this town," he said, staring intently into her face.

He bent down then and picked the ball up from the street. He looked over at the Rockwell house and then back at her. "I guess this is what you were after," he said, handing her the ball Willie had stolen from the Rockwell lawn.

Nellie nodded. "I guess. . . " She couldn't bring herself to make an excuse. He must know the ball was stolen.

"I guess you'd be wise to locate your brother and get home," he said.

She swung around expecting to see Willie behind her, but he was nowhere in sight. Did the man recognize her? Maybe he had seen her with Willie on a different occasion. She turned back, but already he was climbing into his buggy.

"Th-thank you, sir," she called softly, but he didn't

make any sign that he had heard. She watched as he drove away.

She thought for a moment. He seemed so familiar. At Mr. Scalley's—that's where she had seen him. He'd been dressed in overalls and boots, and he'd been bartering his goods—potatoes, turnips, cabbages, maple sugar, crocks of butter, baskets, and brooms. Mr. Scalley had once remarked that he was a fine fella, and honest, "even if he was part Injun."

"Nel?" Willie said, touching her arm. "What you staring at?"

"Nothing, Willie," she said, handing him the ball. She turned back to the Rockwell house. Jennie was taking her place at the piano again, and the beautiful chords of the sonata swelled out into the muggy night. Nellie shook herself and sighed. "Come on, Willie. We'd best be getting home."

Chapter 7

The closer Nellie got to home, the slower she walked. Dread and distaste churned in her stomach like a bout of dyspepsia. Her evening's unhappy experience with the Rockwells and the strange encounter with that man still tormented and clouded her mind. Why did he have to be driving by at the moment she had darted into the street? Wasn't it his fault as much as Willie's or her own that the Rockwells had seen her? And now she was almost home—and Ma would be waiting.

Beside her, Willie whistled softly, happily pressing his newly acquired ball to his chest. Why couldn't she just go along with whatever life ladled up, the way Willie did?

She and Willie had come to Shanty Hill now. Gone were the splendor and grace of the pretty houses and lawns and sweet-smelling bushes. Here weeds struggled to grow in the beaten-down plots of barren earth. A waning moon shone pale through wisps of cloud. The row of shanties leaned crookedly in the long shadows of eerie light.

Nellie dropped down on a pile of rocks that Pa had started making into a wall. As with everything else he started, Pa hadn't had the gumption to finish it. She stared up at the house. The door stood open, but no light, not even a faint flicker of a kerosene lamp with the wick turned down, pushed back the yawning darkness.

How far away the radiance of the great room at the Rockwells' seemed! Here all was clothed in mourning. The shanty was set down under the shadow of a cliff, just above the bank of the river. In the mornings, sunshine merely bounced off the roof, and when it finally came around again late in the day, it was soon swallowed up by the opposite hill. Even in summer the two rooms of the shanty were dark and dank, the air heavy with the odor of kerosene and coal. No natural warmth or comfort was found here.

Willie sat down beside her and nudged her arm. "Nel, what you stopping for?" he asked.

"Ma's not likely gone to bed yet, Willie," she said.

"There's no light," Willie said, tossing the ball up and catching it.

"What are you hurrying for?" she asked. "Something special waiting for you?"

"Nothin' special," he said slowly.

Neither spoke for a minute. Nellie listened to the gentle gurgling of the river and the whispering of the current as it slipped past. How soothing its song! If only she could rush along with it.

"Nel?" Willie said. "Nellie!" he said sharply, breaking into her thoughts.

"Hmm?" she said, pulling herself out of her dream.

"Did that man hurt you?"

Nellie reached up and took the rosebud from her hair. Already it was beginning to wilt. Her shoulders sagged. "No, Willie," she said, swallowing hard. She slipped the flower down into her pocket. "He reined up his horse. I was only taken by surprise. . . . Willie? Did you see the Rockwells out on the porch?"

Willie shook his head.

"You must've heard all the yelling, and Horatio calling out?"

Willie slumped against her side and hung his head. "I ran around and climbed over the fence behind the house. I heard some hollering, but I was afraid to come out of the bushes, and then it got quiet so I peeked through the leaves. The man was climbing into his buggy."

"Did he see you?"

Willie sat up and looked at her face. "No, course not. Why?"

"No reason." She chewed her lip. "Willie, we can't

ever go back to the Rockwells' again. It was horrid being found out. And that awful Horatio, he pointed at me and called me a ruffian. I was so shamed, Willie."

"Sorry," Willie muttered. "It's all my fault, ain't it? I shouldna thrown the ball."

"No matter now, Willie. Don't stew over it," she said, ruffling his hair. "Served me right for being mean."

"Mean? I don't really think you're like Ma, Nel."

"Well, I am mean . . . sometimes," Nellie said thoughtfully. Maybe she had been too insistent about spying on the Rockwells. Maybe Willie was right, maybe she *had* acted like Ma. No, she was not like Ma. She wasn't! "I've been thinking, Willie. Tomorrow night, maybe we'll go up to Homer Whyte's. There's so many bushes and trees around his place. If we're real careful, I guess we wouldn't be seen."

"Homer Whyte's?" Willie said softly. Nellie could see his face light up like a street lamp. "Homer Whyte's?" he said again. "Nel, all I want is to see his house up close. It's grand as a castle, I'll bet."

"Promise you won't do any thieving?"

"Promise," Willie said with solemn sincerity.

Willie meant it, too, but as soon as he spotted anything not nailed down proper or locked up, his fingers would itch till he laid hands on it.

32

Willie jumped up suddenly. "Come on, Nel," he said, slapping his arm. "The mosquitoes are feastin' on me something fierce. They're thicker than flies on a horse's rump."

Nellie laughed and swatted the air as a mosquito buzzed near her face. "Come on, then," she said, getting up. Ma would be ready to wallop her for running off, but right this moment she didn't give a lick. She and Willie had made their peace, and that mattered to her more than anything.

When they were a few steps from the house, Nellie stopped and waited as Willie darted off to empty his pockets into an old tin box he'd hidden under some rocks. If only there was a place to hide herself—but there wasn't. And the town grew more dangerous as the night wore on, with gangs of canal boys roaming the streets.

When she got to the stoop, she could hear Pa's snoring and smell the acrid smoke of Ma's pipe drifting out into the muggy heat. Ma was awake all right, waiting for her in the darkness. Nellie took a step backward. She glanced over her shoulder at the street. A gang of canal boys was coming up along the riverbank hooting. She took a deep breath and stepped into the doorway.

She was yanked the rest of the way in by Ma. Instantly her back and shoulders were showered with blows. Nellie threw her arms up to protect her head.

"I'll learn you. I'll learn you yet, girl," Ma said, her hands flailing in rhythm to her words.

Nellie stood quietly. She was not about to let Ma know her pain.

"Stop! Stop it, Ma!" Willie cried out as he came through the doorway.

Ma struck Nellie one last time, then let her arms drop to her sides. "Sit yourself down," she said, pushing Nellie backwards into a chair. "Think you're making a fool of me, roaming around like an animal after dark?" Ma said, her face pushed up close to Nellie's. "Girl, you're the fool. You'll end up worth nothing, traipsing around like a tramp. I'm trying to get you a decent man."

Decent? Nellie shuddered as she remembered the way Callahan had pawed her when Ma had taken her to the dance hall.

"Some daughter you are. You never been nothin' but a thorn in my side," Ma said, blowing tobacco smoke in her face. "You ain't like any of my other girls. Never one of them give me no trouble. Now, why you always fighting me, girl? Well, you can fight me all you want, but you ain't runnin' off again—I'll see to that."

Chapter 8

Willie had already gone to his cot in one corner of the room when Nellie went to bathe her face and arms in the cool water from the wash basin. Ma looked a little like a rat with her long, thin face and beady eyes, and she was just as scary, the girl decided.

Nellie took her rolled-up blanket from the cupboard and spread it out on her cot. Inside her blanket, she kept the rag doll Grammie Bailey had made her and a cloth sack with her other treasures—the *McGuffey Reader* and a locket Willie had given her.

Willie was a lot like Grammie Bailey, what Nellie could remember of her. Grammie had the sweetest voice and tenderest words and always seemed to know when a body needed a hug. How a woman so good could raise a witch such as Ma was unequaled in wonderment. Gently, Nellie retrieved the rosebud from her pocket and pressed it between the pages and back cover of her old reader. She wasn't exactly sure why she wanted to keep the flower. The life had already gone out of it.

"Nel," Willie called softly from across the room. "Did Ma hurt you much?"

"Not much, Willie. Thanks," she said.

In the darkness Willie began to whistle softly, trilling like a songbird, convinced she was fine.

Nellie slipped off her dress and laid it over a chair back. She lay down on her cot and covered up with the thin wool blanket and clutched her doll. Willie couldn't see inside of her—inside where she felt like horses were galloping, their hooves cutting into her heart. Life could be better than this. Hadn't she and Willie seen it, seen the affection among the Rockwells? Hadn't she felt the sweetness of life when Grammie Bailey was alive, felt it in her own finger-tips when she'd played the piano? How could she get even a portion of that goodness for herself and for Willie? One thing she knew for sure, the better life did not come from the dance floor at Liberty Hall.

She was pulled out of her thoughts by voices in the back room. Willie had ceased his whistling, so Ma must think they were both asleep. Ma spoke in a low voice. Then Pa interrupted, his voice louder, urgent with interest and quiet excitement. What could Ma possibly be saying that was important enough to disturb Pa's sleep?

Cautiously, she eased off her cot and tiptoed

across the packed dirt floor to the curtain that separated the two rooms. She stopped still when Ma spoke, her voice severe.

"That girl's crafty as a fox, slippin' away on me," Ma said. "But she ain't gonna outfox me again. I'm still riled over havin' to give those coins back to Callahan."

"He ain't likely to forget her doing him wrong. He'll be watchin' for her," Pa said.

Her do Callahan wrong? Nellie cringed at the memory of his hands grabbing her.

"That's the truth," Ma said. "We gotta prevent that. Can't sell secondhand goods."

"Well, whatcha think about this, woman?" Pa said.

Nellie crouched down in the darkness and leaned closer to the curtain, but Pa wasn't taking any chances. His voice dropped so low that she couldn't make out any of the words. She heard a low chuckle from Ma. "That'd learn her proper and get back me coins."

Ma's words sent a chill clear through her, even though the night was warm. Quietly, she slipped back to her cot, her heart pounding, her stomach churning with fear. What were they going to do to her? She wrapped her thin arms tight about her rag doll and fell slowly into a troubled sleep.

Chapter 9

Daylight slipped through the cracks of the kitchen wall onto Nellie. She opened her eyes and glanced over at Willie. He was asleep still, his arms wrapped snugly around Horatio Rockwell's ball. Dear Willie—even in his sleep he smiled. If only he didn't have such a hunger for other people's things. It drove her half crazy with worry, wondering what would happen to him if Ma married her off. But she wasn't going to let that happen. She was going to make a plan.

Nellie crept from her cot and went to the basin to wash. She scrubbed her face and arms and brushed her hair smooth. In the dark mirror, she could see a fresh bruise casting a shadow across her shoulder. She winced as she lightly touched the sore spot. Why did Ma want so badly to be rid of her? Could a few coins mean that much?

She heard a rustling movement in the other room and Nellie hurried into her dress before Pa came out.

She laid twigs in the firebox, put chunks of coal on top, and started the fire. She was just putting the coffeepot on when Pa came into the room.

"Mornin', girlie," he said. He stood alongside her for a minute at the cookstove and gave her a long, hard look. "You're a sweet-looking child 'bout ready to burst into blossom," he said, pinching a tress of her hair between a finger and thumb. "How old you gettin' to be, girl?"

Nellie tensed as she turned to study Pa's face. He was up to something, something no good, maybe. It wasn't that Pa was ever fierce about things, like Ma; he just never took much notice of anything other than his own self.

"Thirteen, Pa. Only thirteen," she said, lowering her eyes and taking a step away from him.

"Look pretty near sixteen. You ain't lying to your pa?" he asked.

"No, sir," she said.

He grunted. "How soon you be turnin' fourteen?"

Nellie swallowed hard. "July fourth," she said slowly. It was not much more than a fortnight away.

Pa laughed. "I remember now. Nellie—our Independence day baby. . .That year was the beginning of hard luck for us," he said, as if it were her fault somehow. He grunted again and went to the wash basin. Pa was real particular about his moustache and beard. He scrubbed them with soap and water every morning to get the coal dust out. This morning he hummed as he brushed and trimmed his whiskers.

Nellie listened in wonder. When had she last heard Pa so cheerful? Ma could be right cheerful when it struck her fancy, but not Pa; he was always quiet, solemn, seldom smiling. From the corner of her eye, Nellie saw him fingering his moustache, clipping it carefully.

"Coffee's done, Pa," she said, setting it on the table with the leftover cornbread and molasses.

"Willie, wake up and give us a story," Pa called out, scraping back a chair and sitting down at the table.

Willie's head popped up from his cot, his face lit like a match. He didn't seem to question Pa's sudden interest in him, and Nellie couldn't help but smile. She could almost see the wheels and whatnots whirring like a clockwork inside Willie's head.

"Give the boy some coffee," Pa ordered.

Willie had scarcely begun his story of last night's escapades, in which he was the hero capturing the prize, when Ma came out. Ma was usually the last one up. Nellie and Willie saw to the morning chores.

"A mite cooler this morning," Ma said, propping the door open. Fresh air from the hillside swept in. "It's a fine day, all right." She took a deep breath and grinned at Pa as if something real pleasant were about to happen. "I feel lucky today," she said, pouring herself some coffee. She sat down next to Pa and lit her pipe. "My left palm is itchin' like it had a fire stoked in it," she said, chuckling as she flexed her fingers.

Nellie looked at her meager portion of cornbread and tin cup of hot coffee. How could she eat when her stomach was turned inside out with fear? Ma and Pa were up to no good, all right. Why else would Pa be so inquiring of her age? Pay such close attention to her looks? It was not in Pa's nature to notice her at all. And last night Ma had said "You ain't runnin' off again—I'll see to that."

"What you got there, Willie?" Ma asked.

"Captured me a ball," Willie said, shifting his eyes toward his sister.

"Captured?" Ma went into frenzied laughter. "Willie, my own blessed angel, you'll make your old folks powerful rich one day with your capturin' ways," she said, sucking on her pipe again.

Nellie sat quietly at the end of the table and warily studied her folks. Ma was in a charmed mood this morning, but then the prospect of money always made her gleeful. Ma always dreamed about riches, never got past the belief that Pa would one day win a fortune from gambling. Even when they had been forced to move out of their house into this shack, Ma had never stopped believing. But Pa lost more than he won. Strange men had come to their house at all hours to take away furniture, until nothing had been left in their small parlor. Even the Franklin stove had gone in the dead of winter. The men had come and hauled it out with the coals still burning.

"Don't you feel Lady Luck is with us this morning, Pa?" Ma asked.

"I feel durn sure she is, woman," he said, reaching across the table and swiping Nellie's cornbread.

Nellie stared hard at the tabletop. She'd better figure a way to get free of Ma and Pa, and she'd better do it before the day was over.

Chapter 10

The problem, Nellie decided when she and Willie were on their way to get water for the wash, was that she couldn't come up with a plan, at least not a real plan. She couldn't turn herself into anything as wonderful as the "Moonlight Sonata" and drift away above the steepled churches. She couldn't become Jennie Rockwell or old Miss Sutton, her schoolteacher. She was stuck with her poor old self, and she'd best begin somewhere close to home. Willie seemed as reasonable a place to start as any. She'd get his mind set on the idea of freedom; the way he favored western serials, that shouldn't be too hard.

"Say, Willie," Nellie said, dipping her pail into the river. "How'd you figure Ma and Pa being so cheerful this morning?"

Willie set his pail on a rock, a perplexed look crossing his face. "I figure it was right nice for a change," he said. His look became one of suspicion. "How'd you figure it, Nel?"

Nellie shrugged. "I don't know exactly. Just seemed peculiar, like maybe they were conniving some sort of . . . I don't know," she said again, shifting the pail from one hand to the other.

Willie didn't say a word. He grabbed his pail from the rock and filled it with water. That was Willie. He preferred not to complicate life by thinking about it. Maybe that was why he was mostly agreeable.

"Well, don't you think it was peculiar?" she asked as they started back up the riverbank.

He walked a ways ahead and then stopped. He looked up at the shack for a moment and then back at his sister. "Suppose so," he said slowly. "But you don't have to spoil it by announcing that Ma and Pa weren't being agreeable for real."

Nellie stared hard at her brother. "Doesn't it even bother you an ounce?" she asked, sweeping past him.

"Course it bothers me," he said crossly, coming up alongside her. "But there ain't nothing we can do about it."

"Maybe not. Maybe so," she said mysteriously.

Willie jerked his head toward her. "Watcha ya talkin' about, Nel?" They were almost to the house now. Ma was outside pouring hot water into the galvanized washtub.

"I'm talking about freedom, Willie. I aim to be free."

"Free? What you mean, free?" Willie asked. "You're already free. The Constitution says so."

"Maybe it says so, maybe that's the way it's *supposed* to be, but it doesn't make it true," Nellie said. "Tell me, how much say do you figure I have about who Ma gets me hitched up to?"

Willie scuffled his feet and looked down. "It still don't mean you ain't free," he muttered.

"Then what does it mean, Willie?"

Willie looked up and stared at his sister. "Nel, why can't you ever let things be? Why you always have to be pokin' around in my head? All you end up doing is makin' every blessed thing harder."

"I do it because I want you to get free of Ma and Pa . . . with me. You'll never be a newspaper man unless you get away. You'll end up working on the canal, just like all the other boys."

Willie's shoulders drooped.

"But not if we make a plan, Willie."

"What you aim for us to do?" Willie asked.

"Nellie! Willie!" Ma called shrilly. "Hurry up with those pails."

Nellie gave a sigh of relief. For once she was glad to have Ma yell. She might win Willie over with her talk of freedom, but she wasn't about to tell him she had no plan yet, not even an inkling of one. "I'll tell you all about it later," she said, hurrying to the shanty.

They poured the pails of water into the big kettle on the cookstove and went back outside, where Ma was sitting on a three-legged stool shaving soap into the wash water. "Bring me the scrub board, Willie," she said. "I guess we have us enough water now." She looked up at Nellie. "Best change into your other frock and put the one you're wearing and your shift in the tub here. Then I need you to go over to Scalley's, so find a scrap of paper to write a list on."

But Nellie just stood there. "What about the wash?" she asked as Willie came back with the scrub board.

"What about it?" Ma said, taking the board. "Guess I can manage awhile till you get back—that's if you ever get goin'."

"Can you manage without me, too?" Willie asked.

Ma laughed, a most pleasant look coming over her face. Willie could do that to her. "Ready to roam, that's my boy," Ma said. "Well, go on with you. There'll be plenty of chores waitin' when you get back."

Nellie went inside and stripped off her old gingham and undershift. She reached up over her cot and carefully took her dark green calico dotted with tiny pink flowers off the nail. Ma was surely up to something. She never let her skip out like this on wash day, even to go to the grocer's. But what could going to the grocer's have to do with anything?

Nellie pulled the frock over her head and went to the small mirror over the wash basin. She never gave much thought to her looks, but there was something about the calico that made her feel special. Slowly, she did up the fastenings on the dress, watching in the mirror as her eyes deepened in color and her cheeks grew creamy. How could a simple frock change her that much? . . .What if she saw the Indian man bartering at Scalley's today? Would he tip his hat and chat with Willie about the news while she was getting Ma's order filled? What would he think of her, of Willie, after the incident in front of the Rockwells' last night?

"Nellie, get out here, girl!" Ma hollered.

"Coming, Ma," Nellie called, quickly smoothing her hair with her fingers.

Then she gathered up her soiled clothing, took one of Willie's stubby pencils, tore a corner off the front of the *Herald* and hurried back outside.

"*Whit-whoo*," Willie whistled as she dropped her clothes into the washtub.

A smile crept across Ma's face. "You look right pleasing, wearing that calico," Ma said. Something in her face warmed for an instant, and she loosened her grip on the washboard.

Nellie gave her mother a questioning look. But Ma shook herself and the moment passed, her face growing tight again. "Dried beans. Write that down," Ma said. She started in scrubbing the Johnsons' linens again. "Write down molasses and cornmeal, and get a chunk of salt pork. Now go along with you, you're wastin' daylight."

Nellie stuffed the list into her pocket. "Come on,

Willie," she said. But the look on Ma's face wouldn't leave her. Somewhere inside herself Ma *did* care. Didn't she?

Chapter 11

Nellie and Willie walked slowly down the path to the covered bridge. "Willie," Nellie said, when they had crossed over the river and were walking along Second Street, "am I really pretty?"

"Well, sure, Nel," he said.

Nellie chewed her lip. "And do I look grown-up, Willie? Enough to be married off?" she asked anxiously.

Willie shrugged. "Well, you don't need stuffin' in your front no more."

Nellie stopped dead. "I may look different," she said, "but I'm just the same inside. Don't you ever say I'm not." Even as she spoke, she knew she was-n't the same. She was burning with an anger as fierce as the fire that had swept through the cold wooden stores of Front Street last winter.

They were quiet again, surrounded by the bustling noise of town. They strolled down the side street past Patmor Carriage and Wagon Builders and O'Hanley

Saddle and Harness Makers. When they were in front of the large opened doors of O'Connell Brothers Blacksmith and Horseshoer, Willie suddenly stopped.

"Come on, Willie," Nellie said, tugging on his arm. But he broke free and ran into the blacksmith's where a man with a leather apron was hammering an iron shoe on an anvil.

"Mister, mister," Willie called, running up to someone standing near the blacksmith.

Nellie started toward them, her fists clenched at her sides. Then she stopped. She didn't want to create a scene with Willie or draw attention to herself.

She watched as the man tipped his hat. "How are you, lad?" he called in greeting. He rested one hand on Willie's shoulder and steered him away from the coal fires and clanging hammer toward the wide-flung doors. "Ah, so you're not alone," he said as he caught sight of Nellie.

She took a step backward. It was the man who had seen her at Rockwells' last night. "Willie! Come away . . . now!" she said, but Willie ignored her. The problem with Willie was that he would bother any-one who had ever shown him the least bit of atten-tion or kindness.

"No harm," the man said, nodding to her politely. "My horse threw a shoe last night just as I came into town." He directed his speech to her.

"Oh. . ." Nellie could feel her cheeks grow warm.

Did he mean she was at fault? Was he blaming her for the misfortune? "I'm sorry," she said, moving farther away from him and closer to the street.

"No need to be. It's a common enough occurrence," he said. This time, thankfully, he turned away from her and stepped back into the dark interior of the smithy.

"Mister, are you stopping at Scalley's today? That's where we're off to," Willie said.

"No, I'm afraid not, lad. I've other business today," he said. Nellie noted that instead of his usual overalls, he was wearing a well-fitted suit—though not a fashionable one like Mr. Rockwell wore.

Hesitantly, Nellie moved closer to the door. Apparently, the man bore them no ill will, and he seemed not in the least perturbed by Willie's accosting him so boldly. If only somehow she could get Willie away without causing a scene.

She looked at the man for a moment and noticed the darkness of his face, the whiteness of his teeth. His skin was smooth, without whiskers, and he was younger than she had thought the night before.

"Here, take this if you want, lad," he said, removing a folded-up newspaper from under his arm. "You can read about the Haymarket Trials in Chicago." Then he shook his head, turning, it seemed, to include her: "It's a dark hour for the cause of the laboring poor."

Nellie couldn't help but notice Willie's face. Her brother was staring at the man and hanging on his every word as if he were President Cleveland himself.

"Thanks, mister," Willie said, fitting the paper beneath his own arm.

The man smiled. "You'd better go along with your sister now."

Relieved, she nodded her thanks to him as Willie walked over to her. Perhaps their meeting was providential after all. The newspaper would at least provide a distraction and keep Willie occupied and out of mischief while they were at the grocer's.

Chapter 12

Nellie walked quickly away, Willie trailing behind, and turned the corner onto Front Street.

It was then that the sign in the window of Samuel Brothers Tailor Shop caught her eye:

GIRL WANTED

INQUIRE WITHIN

And just like that, a plan fell into place. It was so simple, really. She didn't know how old a girl had to be to work in a proper establishment, but hadn't Pa just said that very morning that she looked sixteen? Sixteen seemed a safe age. She'd say she was sixteen. Nobody could prove different. She stepped toward the large window. She'd never been in a tailor shop before.

"Nel," Willie called. "What you gawking at that old dingy place for?"

"Quick, Willie, come here," she said, motioning with her hand, excitement rising in her voice.

"Whadda you want?" he asked.

"Look," she said, pointing to the sign. "That's my plan."

"That's your plan? Gosh, Nellie, this is freedom?" he said, looking crestfallen. "Thought maybe we'd go out west, become outlaws, rob trains."

Nellie stamped her foot. "Willie, we're not outlaws and we're not bums. I aim to get hired there so I can give Ma my wages, so you can stay in school and be a news reporter," she said. "I'm old enough for hire."

Willie scowled. "You ain't never been in there. What you gonna say to them old men?" he asked, pressing near the glass and peering in.

Nellie grabbed his collar and yanked him away. "Don't go ruining my chances by smearing the window," she said. "And don't worry. I know right well what proper manners are."

"Reckon you're likely to order them to hire you," he said with a grin.

Nellie laughed. "Reckon I will if that's what it takes," she said. "Now sit here and read your paper while you wait."

"Why can't I go with you and read in there?" Willie asked.

Nellie shook her head and took a deep breath. " 'To give a favorable impression, a person should always apply for a position without the encumbrance of packages or children or the company of others.' "

"Sounds like Miss Sutton," Willie muttered.

"Now stay here and stay out of trouble," Nellie said, stepping up on the stone landing. She grabbed the brass knob and pulled open the heavy wood door.

Once she was inside, her bravado vanished, and her heart began to chug like a fired-up locomotive. The only light in the dim interior came from the gas lamps on the walls and daylight filtering through a large window, black with coal dust, at the rear. There were several drab-looking men in aprons and shirt sleeves doing alterations to men's suits.

She smoothed her sweaty palms down over the gathers of her skirt and wet her lips. She had no idea who the proprietor might be. Every man in the shop seemed to be busily engaged. For a moment she thought to turn and flee, but then she reminded herself of the fate that awaited her at the Liberty Dance Hall. Besides, she could never face Willie if she left now.

She stepped toward the counter. "Excuse me, sir," she said boldly, expecting the owner to come forward and greet her. Instead, all the men looked up and stared, blinking like old, tired horses. "Excuse me," she said. "I'd like to speak to the owner about the position—the ad there in the window," she said, gesturing toward the street.

The men blinked some more. Finally, one stood up and shuffled forward, wiping his hands on his apron. He had dark, puffy bags under his eyes.

"The brothers are upstairs in the factory," he said. "They don't like interruption. It'd be better if you came back near closing."

Nellie chewed her lip. It occurred to her that perhaps it was the men working who didn't like interruption. "Please inform the elder Mr. Samuel that Miss Bishop is here about the position. Tell him she refuses to leave until she speaks to him personally." Nellie spoke with a firm voice. Didn't she sound like Miss Sutton though? She leaned against the counter slightly, her legs gone limp as a weeping willow branch.

The man's eyes widened, his brows raised higher and higher. "Guess it'll be the only way to get rid of you," he said wearily.

"You'd be right about that," she said sharply.

He sniffed a little as he walked away up a dark flight of stairs at the rear of the shop. The others had long since bent their backs to their tasks.

In no time at all he returned, followed by a short, round, balding man with a thick moustache that appeared to go clear round his head. The short man was dressed the same as the others, but he moved with the confidence of someone accustomed to respect.

He walked straight up to the counter and without first speaking gave Nellie a long, sweeping look, up and down, his eyes finally resting on her face. He grunted. "You're from Shanty Hill?"

How had he known? Her bare feet? Her Irish name? "Yes," she said, tilting her chin up and holding herself erect.

"You speak well for yourself from what my man says." He looked thoughtful. "Can you do sums? Can you write a good hand?"

Nellie looked straight in his eyes. "Sir, I can do both very well, thank you."

"I believe you can," he said softly, studying her face. He cleared his throat. "Well, you'd have to start in the factory on a machine, but I need a girl with some sense and a head about her for other tasks. I'm willing to give you a try. Payment by the week of six dollars and noon meal supplied. Do you need a room?"

Did she need a room? She thought of Willie, thought of Ma. She wet her lips. She hated the thought of leaving Willie, but with Ma's threat of last night and the air of conspiracy between her folks this morning, she knew she'd better get away. "Mr. Samuel, sir, I could use a room."

He nodded. "One dollar a week taken out of your wages. You'll share a room with another girl. Since it's Saturday noon, no need to report until Monday morning. Be here at six A.M. sharp. I'll show you around the factory then." He reached across the counter and shook her hand firmly. "We're a fine establishment with a reputation for fair labor practices. So be forewarned that no defiance will be tolerated. Good day now." He let go of her hand and turned away.

Nellie stood still at the counter for a moment, watching as he climbed the stairs. She'd done it! She'd gotten herself a proper position! This could cure a multitude of ills for her and Willie.

"Nel," Willie called in a loud whisper.

Nellie whirled around. Willie's head was showing at the dark wood door.

"Willie!" she said, rushing over to him and hustling him out onto the sidewalk. "I got hired, Willie," she said. "I start work the day after tomorrow."

"Does that mean you'll be free?" he asked.

"Maybe," she said. She thought of the tired-looking men, the dark stairway that led to a hidden place, and Mr. Samuel's warning. "Maybe not."

Chapter 13

Mr. Scalley was the most popular grocer for all of Shanty Hill, having the lowest prices, extending the most credit, and in general being convivial in nature. Nellie was thankful that Scalley's was located on South Front Street, well below the center of business activity. It was also well below the Delaware & Hudson railroad station, where coal was brought in from over the mountains and reloaded onto the canal boats. Nellie always tried to avoid the canal and its hard-talking, hard-drinking, hard-fighting men and boys.

"So when are you gonna tell me about your proper position?" Willie asked when they had stopped outside Scalley's.

Nellie glanced up the street toward the canal bridge and the D & H station just as a train whistle blew and the steam from a locomotive rose above the shops. She grabbed her brother's arm. She hated to take Willie inside, where he would fill his pockets if she didn't keep her eyes on him every second. But if she left him to wait on the sidewalk, he'd be lured away by romantic notions of the train, and she'd find him hanging around by the canal.

"Come with me, Willie," Nellie said, pulling him along with her up the steps.

He wrenched his arm free. "The train's in. I'll just go over and watch them unload the coal while you're in Scalley's. I'll stay clear of the men, I promise," Willie said, with a look of pure longing on his face. "Wouldn't it be a real adventure to go out west on a train? I ain't never been on a train."

"That train doesn't go out west, Willie. It just goes back over the mountain to the coal mines," Nellie said, latching onto his arm again. "Come on! We've got to get Ma's order filled and get ourselves home, or I'll get another walloping."

"I know the train don't go out west, but it goes somewheres I never been," Willie said as he followed Nellie, this time without trying to pull free.

A bell clanged harshly when Nellie opened the door. "And one more thing," she whispered, dropping his arm. "Don't you steal from old Scalley, hear? Keep those itchy fingers in your pockets and out of the cracker barrel and the cheese and the pickles."

Willie shoved his hands down into his overall pockets. "That good enough for you?"

Nellie nodded and took a deep breath. "Stay close

to me," she said, walking across the dark wood floor to the counter. She glanced quickly around the inside of the store, but it was deserted. True to his word, the man from last night hadn't come in to barter goods.

"Morning, Mr. Scalley," she said, retrieving the list from her dress pocket.

Mr. Scalley was stocking the shelves behind his counter with small, pricey cans of food that had colored pictures of vegetables and fruits on the labels. Nellie found them most compelling. Mr. Scalley had his back to her and Willie.

"Mr. Scalley, it's Nellie Bishop," she repeated loudly this time, leaning across the counter.

Mr. Scalley turned slowly around, his usual warm smile replaced by a look of annoyance.

Nellie straightened. Had he discovered Willie's thefts? She looked quickly at Willie. His hands were still deep in his pockets, but he was eyeing the row of jars filled with Mrs. Scalley's homemade lollipops.

Nellie looked back at Mr. Scalley and waited for him to speak.

The old man stroked his long white beard. He peered closely at her face and then cleared his throat. "Your ma send you—or your pa?" he asked.

Nellie studied his face. What a strange thing for him to ask. "Why, um, Ma did," she said. "Here's the list." She placed it on the counter in front of him.

Mr. Scalley shook his head. "You're a good girl, Nellie. I've known you since you were a wee bit smaller than Willie there. I know you're a good girl, but. . ." He stopped and placed both hands on the counter and leaned over closer to her.

"But . . . what?" she said. He had found out about Willie. What was he going to do to them?

"But I can't extend you any more credit. Your folks are nine months behind in their bills now. I told your ma yesterday, told her I couldn't. Told her in no uncertain terms, I did," Mr. Scalley said, frowning.

"Ma was here yesterday?" Nellie said slowly. "Ma knew? But then why . . ." She stopped and looked away from his face. Why had Ma sent her to Scalley's?

Mr. Scalley searched her face. "Sorry. I'm sorry as can be, Nellie. It was mean and low-down for her to send you here," he said, a pained look coming into his eyes. "Wish I could help, but . . . "

"But, Mr. Scalley," Nellie said, thinking of the empty shelves at home. She straightened and looked him in the eye. "I've been hired by Samuel Brothers. I start work on Monday. I'll pay you back."

"Right pleased I am that you've found a position, but I ain't about to burden a girl with her folks' debt, and the debt has to be paid—or no more credit."

Nellie nodded, her face burning with shame. "Sorry to have bothered you," she said, turning away from the counter. "Come on, Willie. We'd best get back." She walked toward the door with Willie beside her.

"I'm real sorry. Ain't nothing personal," Mr. Scalley called after them.

"Personal enough," Nellie muttered. She gave the door a hard yank, the bell clattering rudely in her ears. But truthfully, she knew that old Scalley had been fair and that he *was* sorry, at least for her. It was his look of pity that made her angrier than anything. It was not a look anyone would ever have given Jennie Rockwell.

Chapter 14

"What're you gonna do?" Willie asked, as if this were a problem she had created. He hurried to keep up with her long strides. "Ma ain't gonna like it."

Nellie stopped in the middle of the sidewalk and grabbed Willie and whirled him around to face her. "Stop talking like a Shanty Hill boy. How are you ever going to be a newspaper man if you keep talking that way?"

"Do this. Do that. Why can't you ever let me be?" Willie asked, jerking free of her grasp.

"Sorry, Willie," she said, deflated. They started walking more slowly. "I don't know what I'm going to do. I can't figure why Ma sent us to old Scalley in the first place."

"Maybe Ma thought you'd soften up old Scalley and he'd give us a little something," Willie said, swinging his arms. He didn't seem a bit troubled.

They were over on Second Street now and almost to the covered bridge. "Maybe," Nellie said, worriedly. "Maybe not," she added quietly. The occurrences of the day had all been peculiar, like a sudden change in musical key—Pa taking such an interest in her looks, Ma making her change into the calico and letting her go off to the grocer's before the wash was done . . . and then the whole business with Mr. Scalley. She shook her head in bewilderment as her stomach coiled into a knot of fear.

"I'm hungry," Willie said. "How about you?"

"Not much," she said, lying, as they passed through the cool shade of the bridge.

"Would you like some cheese?" he asked, offering her a chunk.

"Oh, Willie," she said with annoyance. It was no use. How could she ever get him safely grown up?

"Well?" he asked, waving the strong cheddar under her nose.

Her stomach rumbled noisily, and her mouth watered. She'd had no food that morning, and the look and smell of the cheese made her weak with hunger. "I can't," she said, shaking her head.

"Better eat it," Willie said. "How you gonna work for Samuel Brothers if you don't eat?"

She sighed and took the cheese he was holding out in front of her. She hated herself for being so weak, but once she was earning a fair wage, she'd see to it that Willie had food enough to keep him from stealing it. She started to nibble the cheese slowly to make it last longer, but then couldn't resist gulping it down in one big bite.

As they walked up the narrow dirt path to Shanty Hill, Willie spoke, his mouth still full of cheese. "Suppose Ma will be wrathful."

"Can't be helped," Nellie said, heading toward their shanty.

Ma was hanging wash, and Nellie hurried over to help her.

"Don't see no provisions," Ma said. "You were gone mighty long, too."

Nellie wet her lips. "Mr. Scalley said—he said we couldn't have any more credit until our debt was paid."

"And it ain't Nel's fault," Willie added, poking his head between the linens.

Ma shook her head. "If that girl had've listened to me, if she'd gotten hitched like I wanted, we'd be outta debt. Now, I'd like to know how it ain't her fault?" she said, going to sit on the stool by the wash-tub.

Nellie sucked in her breath and grabbed up a shirt from the basket. "I got myself a position with Samuel Brothers. Five dollars a week I'll be paid, and that'll be a lot more than you could get marrying me off to some fool drunk." She shoved the clothespins down hard, making the line dance.

"Five dollars a week?" Ma said slowly. "That's more

than I git for washing." She narrowed her eyes and jammed the stem of her pipe into her mouth. "Did you tell old Scalley that?"

"I told him, Ma. He said no credit till the debt is all paid up."

Ma shook her head. "Never thought old Scalley would turn on one of his own kind." She sighed deeply and puffed on her pipe. "You'll have to go look up your pa and get some coins off him."

"Over to the canal?" Nellie asked in surprise.

Ma looked up and squinted at the sun. "By this time of day, he'll be at Reilly's. Yup, you'll have to go fetch some coins to pay Scalley. Your pa's likely to have won some by now. You know my palms was itchin' this morning. It's a true sign," she said, chuckling. "Now go, go on with you, soon as you hang up that last piece there."

"Pa doesn't allow us in the taverns," Nellie said, studying Ma's face.

Something sly flickered in Ma's eyes. "Don't worry. Me and your pa already talked it out last night," she said smoothly.

Nellie lifted the last shirt from the basket and pinned it slowly as she watched Ma puffing her pipe and staring peacefully at the river. What was going on? When had she ever known Ma not to wallop her? And it wasn't true—Pa wouldn't be in Reilly's this early. She'd just seen the train pulling into the station, and that meant the canal men would be real busy. Besides, Pa never permitted her and Willie in the saloons; he said that it was shameful for a man to have his folk coming after him, which suited her just fine. She never fancied the likes of the saloons Pa frequented or the company he kept.

A sick feeling started in her stomach and spread through her arms and legs. It was plain that Ma and Pa had brewed up some iniquitous plan; it was hanging in the air as thick and nasty as Ma's pipe smoke.

Chapter 15

"I don't like it. I don't like it one bit," Nellie fumed as she and Willie began the trek back into town. "Ma and Pa are up to no good."

For once, Willie seemed troubled too. "Why would she send us to Reilly's after Pa, Nel?" Willie asked. "Pa won't be there, and if he is, he'll be wrathful sure enough."

"I don't know, Willie," she said, stopping to look at her brother. There was real fear in his eyes.

"Something bad, you think?" he whispered.

"Most likely," she said, chewing her lip. "I heard Ma and Pa talking last night after you'd gone to sleep. I couldn't hear all of it, but I heard enough. Pa cooked up some scheme, and Ma was real pleased. It has to do with me, Willie. Something about me. Something that will get coins in that old witch's fingers."

"I don't know what else Ma could do, besides

them dances," Willie responded with a frown.

They walked quietly together along the narrow road and back through the covered bridge.

"Here's something good," Willie said, pulling two lint-covered lollipops from his pocket. He held one out to her.

"Oh, Willie, how much did you steal from old Scalley?" she said, taking the candy. She dearly loved sweets, and it was a rare occasion to get any. She stuck it in her mouth and then smiled. It was anise, the flavor of the licorice candy Grammie Bailey used to give her. Even when he was doing wrong, Willie thought to please her. "What kind do you have?"

"Same," Willie said. "Wanna go to Public Square until we finish them?"

"Public Square?" Nellie looked up Second Street. She shook her head. "Might be ladies out strolling. They wouldn't think it fitting for us to be there. We'll just walk slow," she said. It might be grand to stop and watch the ladies from a distance; they seemed so confident in their pretty clothes, so carefree in their chatter. But Nellie didn't even suggest it. After last night at the Rockwells', she didn't want to be seen even looking toward such fine folk.

They walked farther along Second Street this time so as not to pass by Scalley's once they got to Front. Nellie wasn't exactly sure where Reilly's was located—there seemed to be more taverns in the town than all the other establishments put together—but she had an idea Reilly's would be close to the Canal Basin Bridge. When they turned the corner of Race, Willie slowed almost to a stop.

"What if we don't go?" he asked. "What if we just go back and say we couldn't find Reilly's, or that they wouldn't let us in?"

Nellie bit down on one side of the lollipop and crushed it with her teeth. Suppose they did disobey Ma, then what? Then she and Willie would surely be beaten. "We still need food, Willie. Ma and Pa are up to no good, but we have to eat."

Willie's shoulders sagged. "Let's get it over with then," he said.

Already the morning fog had burned off, and the day was turning steamy hot. As Nellie and Willie walked along Front Street across from the canal, the mugginess and the smell of horses pressed against them. They made their way slowly, peering up at the name on each building for Reilly's Saloon. Willie spotted it first. "There," he said, pointing to the weathered sign over the entrance.

Just as Nellie had expected, the saloon was located right next to the Basin Bridge. She stared at the front of Reilly's and sucked nervously on what was left of her lollipop. "I can't go in there," she said. "Only men are allowed in those places."

"You can too go in—you have Ma's permission.

Besides, you've got to. Ma will wallop you if you don't."

Silently, she and Willie stared at the saloon door as if Pa might lurch out any second.

"I'd best go in alone, Willie. I'll just tell Pa my errand, then I'll be right back out. So don't worry." She started toward the building to show Willie she was not afraid, but it was hard to keep her legs from shaking long enough to move forward.

"Psst . . . Nel," Willie said, coming up behind her and pointing down the street. "Look, it's the man who gave me the paper—coming out of the bank."

She looked down the street nervously. "Willie, stay here. Don't go running off and pestering him again." The man was walking up the block in their direction. She pulled Willie over to the step. She couldn't let that man see her—not now.

Fingers of heat spread up her neck and across her face. She dropped her gaze and scurried up the steps to the door.

"Wait, Nellie," Willie cried, grabbing ahold of her skirt. "I'll go with you."

"No!" She shook her head. "Pa won't hurt me, Willie, you know that. Besides, it's not going to be like this forever. Starting Monday, things will be different. Now sit down on the step here. I'll be right back." Without another word or a backwards glance, she opened the door of Reilly's Saloon and stepped inside.

Chapter 16

Nellie flattened herself against the door and squinted into the dim light of Reilly's Saloon. The air was thick with the smells of cigar smoke and whiskey and the sounds of great laughter and clamorous voices.

Pa seemed to notice her presence immediately. "Come here, girl!" he called out through the haze of smoke, his words slurring.

Nellie breathed deeply and swallowed back her fear. She didn't want Pa to see how she was shaking with fright. Slowly, she stepped forward into the crowded room. As she moved through the forest of men toward Pa's table, the great laughter fell, and the voices grew still. Nellie could feel every eye turned upon her.

"This here's my girl, men," Pa hollered out into the quiet. "Sweet, unspoilt heifer," he said with a grand wink and a guffaw. "To my girl," he said, raising a glass to his lips. He drank, letting the liquid spill from the sides of his mouth and dribble down his face.

Other glasses clinked, and the raucous laughter pressed hotly against her. She kept her face directed toward Pa. He must have been here a good while—already his eyes were heavy-lidded and his voice thick from too much drink. She was grateful now for the smoke that hung in the air; surely Pa would see her loathing otherwise.

"Purty sweet looking," a voice near her said, and she pulled away as fingers crawled onto her arm. Inside her, she felt the fire of her anger and revulsion flare up as it had when Callahan had pawed her at the Liberty Dance Hall. She stopped by the table where Pa was playing cards and stood near his chair. "Ma sent me," she said, in a calm, measured voice that hid her inner quaking. "Ma said I should ask you for some coins."

"She did, did she?" Pa said in a jovial manner, as if they were friends. He reached into his pocket and pulled out several dimes, some five-cent pieces, and a half-dollar. "Take it all, hear?" he said, putting it into her hand. "Givin' you my last cent, girl. Hear that, me very last cent, men. A man's gotta keep his family fed," he said, patting her arm.

When had Pa ever cared if she had food or not? Nellie wanted to shake off his touch, fling the coins down on the table, and run out, but she didn't.

"Thanks, Pa," she said mildly. It didn't make any

sense. Why was he being so generous, talking as if he were glad to have her in this private world of his that had always before been forbidden?

"Run along now. Tell your ma I'll have more coins than she can count by tonight," he said, blowing rings of cigar smoke into the air. "Tell her me palms is itchin'!"

"Yes, Pa," Nellie said. She closed her fingers over the handful of coins and made for the door. Was it possible Pa was on a winning streak? Surely a good win would make Pa agreeable and even generous. Still, she hadn't imagined his and Ma's conniving words the night before nor the smug glint in Ma's eyes this morning. If it was their notion to get her to the dance, she'd kick and claw and snarl at any man who dared approach.

She was so intent upon getting safely through the throng of men around her that she bumped into someone who was stepping through the doorway of the saloon.

"Pardon me," she said, then found herself looking up into the face of the man who had nearly run her over the night before. Nellie pushed past him and reached for the door.

He grabbed her wrist just as her fingers circled the knob.

"Please," she said, trying to yank her arm free, "let

me go." But his strong fingers held her fast. Why, he was no better than her pa, frequenting such places as this!

"Willie said. . . . I wanted to make sure you were safe." His voice was low-pitched and resonant.

"Oh." She searched his face. His brown eyes were warm with compassion—or was it pity? "I don't need your help. I don't need anyone's help," she whispered fiercely, ashamed of being so needy, of being seen in such a place as Reilly's.

Pa's drunken voice boomed out in the background. "Ain't got no money, men. What'll I wager now?"

Nellie shivered. What would he wager? A dance and squeeze with his daughter? She had to get out before Pa saw her and called her back. "Sir, I can take care of myself," she said hotly.

The man wrinkled his brow and released her arm. "You shouldn't be trying to fend for yourself in this town."

"But I have to!" she cried out, almost sobbing.

He moved aside and thrust open the door for her, with a sweep of his arm toward the street.

Chapter 17

Nellie brushed by him and out into the light. The darkness of the saloon and the stranger were both swallowed up by the closing door.

"Uh oh," Willie said as he looked at her face. "Guess it was a good thing that dark stranger came to help you out. Just like in a western, huh?"

"Not like in a foolish newspaper serial," Nellie spat out. "I told you I'd be fine." She grabbed his shoulder. "What did you say to him?"

Willie gave a great sigh. "Ma's right. You're the prickliest thorn. Can't never help you."

"Well, I didn't need his help. If I'm going to be independent, then I have to fight my own battles," she said in defense. "Come on. We'd better get these coins to Ma." She jingled the change in her hand and started down the street.

"Coins?" Willie said, coming right up alongside her, all other matters forgotten. "Pa gave you coins? You're not clownin'?"

Nellie shook her head, her lips pressed tightly together.

"Show me then. Show me," he begged.

"When we get to Second Street," Nellie said. "Too many people. I don't want anyone to see."

Willie nodded, and they hurried away from the crowd and bustle of Front Street. As soon as they turned the corner, Willie stopped. "Let's see, Nel. Let me hold them, will you?"

Nellie opened her fist and clinked the coins, one at a time, into Willie's outstretched hand, laughing as his eyes grew round with wonder.

He whistled softly. "My palms is itchin' like a poison ivy rash," he said, and then added, "I'm gonna get rich, I can feel it!" He twitched his head like Ma. "Must be something to it, Nel."

"Something to it. Something bad, like an epidemic of cholera, maybe," Nellie muttered, watching as Willie counted the coins. If only she could put the pieces together the way her fingers had so easily played the right chords on the old school piano.

"One dollar and fifty-five cents," Willie said, curling his fingers and making a tight fist over the coins. "You know what we could buy with this at Paterson's?" He rolled his eyes, and Nellie could almost see the visions of toys and confections whirling in his head.

"We could buy us a walloping, too," Nellie said.

"I was only pretendin'," Willie muttered.

Nellie lowered her eyes. "Sure, Willie," she said, sorry that she'd spoiled his moment. "Why don't you carry the coins to Ma?"

Willie flashed her a smile. "Really, Nel?"

She nodded. "Jingle them in your pocket and feel rich for a while," she said, starting slowly down Second Street toward the covered bridge.

Willie walked beside her, whistling softly. For a few minutes they didn't speak. Then Willie said, "Say, Nel, what was it like in Reilly's? Did Pa get wrathful?"

She shrugged and quickly decided against telling how Pa had called her a heifer. "No, he was agreeable enough for Pa."

"And he gave you the coins—just like that?" Willie asked, snapping his fingers.

Nellie snapped her fingers back at him. "Just like that," she said. Maybe Pa had given permission for her to go into the saloon just to get men to the dance, men who could pay Ma coins. Could that be it?

"We can't go home," Willie said, as if the thought had just taken shape in his head. He jingled the coins in his pocket nervously. "Not yet. Not till later, maybe after dark. Maybe not then."

"You can't keep the coins, Willie," she said.

"It's not about the coins. Please, Nel, just let me have a say for once," he pleaded.

Nellie studied Willie's face. His brows were drawn together as if he'd latched onto some powerful thought. "Sure, Willie, sure," she said, wondering what notion had struck him.

They crossed the street and walked past the Episcopal Church and through the gates of the park. It wasn't often that they entered Public Square. The gates and the surrounding fence, the monuments, the fountain and flowers, and the imposing brick face of the courthouse towering over it all with eyes of stern justice implied to Nellie that Public Square was private, designed for a certain class of people that she and Willie were not a part of.

Once inside the park, Nellie glanced cautiously about. The afternoon was hot and the park deserted, except for two men in somber suits walking at the far end. Subdued, she followed her brother. When they came to the Civil War monument, Willie flopped down in its shadow. Nellie sat with her back against the smooth granite base and crossed her arms over her chest. "Well, come on. Have your say now, Willie," she said.

Nervously, Willie ran his tongue over his upper lip. "I think we'd best run away," he said.

"Is this about the train and going out west again?" she demanded. "Because if it is . . ."

"It ain't exactly," Willie said, moving over next to

her. "And it ain't—isn't—about coins. It's about freedom, Nel, like you been sayin'.""

"I don't aim to get freedom by running away," Nellie said. "I got my freedom coming to me right here, starting Monday at Samuel Brothers."

She stared as the two men made their way toward the fountain. One of the men kept nervously glancing behind him. "Ma and Pa may have some wicked scheme, but what can they do?" Nellie continued. She was struck by this truth. As soon as she started working for Samuel Brothers, Ma and Pa couldn't force her to go to Liberty Hall ever again.

"Don't you see? They can't do anything!" she exclaimed.

Willie scowled and slowly traced a finger over the names on the granite. "They can do plenty . . . maybe. You said yourself that Pa's in on it."

As Willie spoke, Nellie caught a movement from the corner of her eye and heard the crunch of pebbles near the white flowering rosebushes. She turned around and was startled to see that the taller of the somber-suited men was alone, watching her and Willie. And he was none other than Mr. Rockwell!

She drew in her breath. What if he remembered her face? But he didn't look angry—just troubled. He was much older and more gaunt-looking in the harsh sun than he had appeared in the warm light of his home. They could easily outrun him if the need arose.

She pressed on Willie's shoulder. She could feel him tense beside her. Yes, Willie knew who it was. Please don't run, Willie, she silently begged, as Mr. Rockwell walked toward them.

" 'To be, or not to be: that is the question,' " he said as he came forward. He stopped just a few short feet from them and stared almost blankly from one to the other. " 'To be, or not to be'—what is the answer?" He shook himself from his trance. "May Lady Luck smile kindly on us all," he said sadly. He touched the brim of his hat and then turned and walked away from them, out through the gates and into the street.

Nellie stared after him and then back at Willie in wonder. "What do you suppose he meant? What troubles could possibly beset a man such as Mr. Rockwell?"

Willie shook his head. "He's gone daft, Nel. Clean off his rocker. Good thing, too. I half expected him to drag us off to the courthouse."

"Why would he say that?" It troubled her that a man such as Mr. Rockwell would make mention of Lady Luck the same way Ma had that morning. Surely Mr. Rockwell was an upstanding man free of such vices as gambling. "He can keep his Lady Luck. I would much prefer that Miss Sutton's Providence was with us today."

Chapter 18

Nellie stopped by the entrance of Public Square and waited for Willie to catch up. He didn't seem at all willing to leave the park. And she didn't like the look of stubbornness and determination on his face. Had she made a mistake in sharing her plan for independence? Now he seemed filled with romantic notions of freedom and adventure.

"Willie, come on," she called. Ma would be fired up like a steam locomotive by the time they got home. "Hurry, Willie. Ma's going to be wrathful," she said in a warning voice.

"Don't care," Willie said as he came through the gates. "I ain't going home. I got a plan o' my own."

Nellie could feel the color drain from her face. She grasped Willie's shoulders tightly and stared into his eyes. "Willie, there's nothing I care more about than you. Please, don't run away. I'll look after you here. I promise."

Willie didn't try to pull free. "Nel, I ain't goin'

back there—and you shouldn't either," he said without blinking.

"Willie, I can't go. Mr. Samuel hired me in good faith. I've got an obligation," she said, her arms dropping limply to her sides.

"You think Mr. Samuel can't get another girl if you don't show? I'm running away, Nel, and you can come or you can stay."

"You can't. I won't let you," she said, lunging at him. But Willie had already turned to run down Race Street toward the canal and the train. "Willie, come back!" she cried as she ran after him.

She could see Willie already darting among the carriages on Front Street as she ran down the side street. Then he disappeared from her sight. Without more than a fleeting thought to what she was doing, she darted across the street and down the alley between the foundry and the flour mill to the train tracks. The locomotive hissed with steam, and the wheels began to turn and rumble.

"Willie! Willie!" she shouted, running alongside as the engine picked up speed. "Willie!" she cried, looking up and down the tracks. Was he on the train? Where was he? "Willie!" she called out again, her voice breaking.

At that moment, Willie poked his head out from one of the empty cars and motioned to her. "Nel, jump on," he mouthed.

"Willie!" she cried, running after the train, but the distance between her and Willie grew by carriage lengths. Then the train veered sharply to the left, where the tracks were caught between the steep bank of the mountain and the river's edge, and she couldn't follow.

Chapter 19

Nellie stood watching helplessly as the tail end of the train rattled along and disappeared around another bend. Her arms dropped limply to her sides. Willie was gone. Her throat ached with unshed tears. What had possessed him to do such a thing? The answer, she realized, was that she had put these notions of independence into Willie's head—and he had turned it into some wild game of adventure. With coins in his hand, his dreams had all seemed suddenly within grasp.

Willie. She stared at the bend where the train had disappeared and hoped that he would suddenly appear. She was still breathing hard from the chase; her bodice clung to her, and her feet and legs were blackened with coal dust from the track bed. Wearily, she shook out the folds of her skirt and brushed them smooth with her hands. What should she do? How could she go home now with no Willie and no money?

She pushed the sweaty locks back from her forehead and squinted up at the sun. It was getting lower in the sky, and the shadows were growing tall around her. She started walking slowly along the tracks, back toward the center of town. It was strange to be alone, hard to remember a time when Willie hadn't tagged along. Oh, Willie. What would become of him?

"Hey, you," a rough voice called.

Startled, Nellie looked up. She'd been so caught up in her misery that she'd failed to notice just how far she'd walked along the tracks. Now here she was, trapped by the canal basin on one side and the stockpile of anthracite on the other. In front of her loomed the leering faces of several canal men.

"Why lookee here," a beefy, red-haired man said, throwing his shovel into a wheelbarrow full of coal. He came toward her. "We got us some extree pay."

Nellie backed away, glancing wildly over her shoulder for the alleyway.

"Why, it's that mean filly, Nellie Bishop," the man said. He spat tobacco juice at her feet, his face becoming hard like a chunk of coal. "Remember me?"

How could she forget Callahan's mauling hands at Liberty Hall and how she'd spit in his face? But Nellie shook her head and backed up several more steps.

"Liar. I ain't fond of liars, and I don't take kindly to high-horse shenanigans from no Shanty Hill slut.

I'm gonna get you, filly, hear? You ain't fighting free of me this time. I got lots of room and lots of help." With that, he bolted forward and grabbed her.

A cheer went up among the men, and as their voices rose, Callahan grinned and turned toward the crowd that was moving in for a better look.

In that second, Nellie mustered all her strength and twisted away from him, ripping the cloth of her bodice as she turned. She ran without a backwards glance, ran with the feeling that Callahan's breath was hot at her back. She heard shouts and pressed forward even harder. She knew she had beaten him when the shouts turned to jeers and then to laughter, but she didn't stop running until she was all the way across Front Street.

Wearily, she leaned against the lamppost on the corner near the jewelry shop to catch her breath. Her bodice had been ripped to the waist, exposing her flesh. Hastily she pulled the material over her and held it fast with one hand. How had she ever believed she could be free? Nellie, the Independence Day baby? She longed for Grammie suddenly, for those old careworn arms to lift and hold her. But Grammie was dead now, and Willie was gone.

"Slattern," a voice hissed nearby.

Nellie looked up as a lady escorted by a fine gentleman alighted from a carriage. They swept by her, the lady pulling her skirts away.

Nellie stared after them, stung by what the young, sweet-faced girl had said, the same sort of word Callahan had spat out only moments before. Lady Luck wasn't smiling kindly on her, and it seemed Providence had deserted her, too.

Bitterly, she held her dress closed and walked down Irving Street toward Second, past Whitney's Livery and the National Hotel. The whole day seemed a jumble in her mind.

She made her way quickly through the covered bridge and then more slowly up the narrow road to Shanty Hill. What would Ma do when she learned Willie had run off? As she approached the path to their shack, she caught sight of a buggy parked in the road. It was apparent that Pa's winning streak had failed, and now men were coming to take away whatever they could lay hands on. As she walked up the path, she expected to see the cookstove being hauled out—for what else was left that could be wagered?

Chapter 20

Nellie stared at Pa sitting hunched over the table. What had his no-count gambling cost them this time? She looked to Ma for the answer.

Ma's face was grimly set. "This here's Jefferson Martin," she said, wrapping her arms tight about her sunken chest. "He's come to fetch you away." The man stepped out of the shadowy interior into the daylight from the open door.

Nellie caught her breath and took a step backward. "So that's your name, Mr. Jefferson Martin, sir." She pulled herself up straight and glared at him. "Who do you think you are, coming to fetch me away? I'm not going anywhere with you. Like I told you before, I can take care of myself." Her heart lurched like a spooked horse. How dare he come into their quarters to fetch her? She couldn't believe that she had actually thought him decent. She held an arm across her chest to hide the ripped cloth of her garment. "You have no right, no right to come here after me," she said through clenched teeth.

Mr. Martin stood with his hat in his hands. "Should I come back after you have some time alone with her?" he asked, addressing Ma.

"No," Ma said spitefully. "It's best done and over with."

"What, Ma?" Nellie asked.

"What do you think, girl?" Ma said. "Your pa wagered you in a poker game and lost. You ain't none of ours now." Ma's eyes were steady. "You have to go with him. You belong to him now."

Nellie caught her breath. What did Ma mean? How could she *belong* to him? She stared at Pa in disbelief. "What do you mean?" she cried.

"It was the woman's doin'," he muttered at the tabletop.

Nellie turned slowly toward Ma. "You old witch," she said with firm resolve.

Ma's face paled, but she didn't flinch. "It be your own doin', girl. You been nothing but a festering thorn to me."

Willie was right. She had no say about what was happening to her; she was nothing more than a slave being passed to a new owner. Why hadn't she run away with Willie? At least they would still be together.

"Go on, get your things. Be quick about it," Ma said, giving her a push.

She turned away from them all, her mind and body stunned as if Ma had struck her. She had to think. She had to work out one problem at a time. First she had to get away from Mr. Martin, and then she had to figure out how to get Willie back. "Please, Ma, let me change into my old gingham."

Ma's gaze swept across her, taking in the torn dress and coal-streaked legs. "Didn't get yourself spoilt down by the canal?"

"No, Ma."

"You got the coins Pa gave you?"

Nellie shook her head. Ma hadn't even asked where Willie had gotten to. All she was interested in was the money. "I gave them to Willie."

"They're good as gone then, foolish girl. Go on, change and be gone 'fore Willie comes."

Willie wasn't coming, but Nellie was not about to tell. She got her small cloth sack, the one with her treasures, and the doll from Grammie Bailey. As she changed from the torn garment to the familiar worn one, she began to work out a plan.

She wouldn't go with that Jefferson Martin. She'd go down to the buggy with him like a horse nuzzling for a lump of sugar, and then she would run. He couldn't fetch her anywhere if he couldn't catch her. She finished hooking her bodice, then wiped her legs clean with the torn dress and smoothed her hair as best she could. She rolled the calico into a bundle with her sack; she could mend the dress and keep it still for good. Her heart thudded wildly, but she pulled aside the curtain calmly and stepped into the kitchen. "I'm ready," she said, her head held high as she swept past Ma to Mr. Martin and stood beside him. "We can leave now."

Mr. Martin nodded to Ma but turned away from Pa as if the other man had been afflicted with a disfiguring disease. He and Nellie walked out of the close, foul air of the shack into the late afternoon sun.

Chapter 21

After stepping over the doorsill, Nellie moved cautiously away from Mr. Martin and down the path toward the buggy with her small bundle. Then she began to walk faster, and when she got to Pa's abandoned wall, she ran.

In town she slowed to a walk, since the streets were beginning to empty of their daytime commotion and she didn't want to draw undue attention to herself. Still, she was aware of Mr. Martin, of the slow clomping of his horse, and the sudden halt if the buggy got too near her.

She had to get inside Samuel Brothers before Mr. Martin knew what she was doing. She'd throw herself on their mercy, beg for the night's lodging. Jefferson wouldn't come after her there. What could he say? How could he prove she was his property? She'd lie. She'd say she'd never seen him before, that he had been following her. He didn't have a paper in writing, a bill of sale, did he? *Did he?*

Once she'd passed the O'Connell Brothers black-smith shop, she broke into a run. She raced the rest of the way down the side street, past McKanna's Cooperage, and around the corner onto Front Street.

She glanced at the window of Samuel Brothers as she hurried up to the door and was surprised to see the "Girl Wanted" sign still in the window. She pulled frantically at the brass knob, but the shop had closed for the day. She banged on the door with her fists. Surely someone was still inside. But if so, no one came to the door. She had failed.

She dropped down on the step, clutching her bundle against her, and wept. It was too much. She had no strength left to fight. She kept her head down, letting the tears flow as she listened to the footfalls of her owner. It was all over. She hadn't beaten anyone. She was the one who had lost.

Mr. Martin came and stood quietly beside her. "I mean you no harm. I'm not going to hurt you, Nellie Bishop. I'll look out for you. Your brother can come along, too, if that's the trouble."

Nellie wiped her eyes and looked up at him. "Willie can't come. Willie's gone and run off on the train. If I'd listened to him, I'd be there, too. I'll never see him now—not ever again."

"How long ago was that?" Mr. Martin asked.

"About four o'clock," Nellie said. "I noticed the time on the clock of the Presbyterian Church."

He took a timepiece from his vest pocket, and his face grew thoughtful. "Over an hour," he said slowly, staring at the face of his watch. "Perhaps we can get Willie back, but we'll have to hurry and telegraph the next station before the train arrives."

Suspicious, Nellie studied his face. Did he mean it? Was he really willing to help her get Willie back? She rocked nervously on the edge of the landing and clutched her bundle. She wanted to trust him, and a part of her did—he'd seemed so tolerant of Willie, and old Mr. Scalley had said he was a good and honest man—but another part of her was afraid, afraid that this was only a trick to get her into his buggy. She had to get Willie back. "I'll walk," she said. "The station's just up the street."

"You can trust me. You know that, don't you?" he asked earnestly.

She turned her face away. "No, I don't," she said.

"I don't suppose you would," he said heavily, slipping his watch back into his pocket. Then he stood up. "We'll both walk. It's just as easy to leave my buggy hitched here."

Nellie glanced quickly at the Samuel Brothers shop before she moved away from the landing. It troubled her that the "Girl Wanted" sign was still in the window.

She had to nearly run to keep up with the long strides of Mr. Martin as they walked swiftly along the boardwalk past the shops of town. The shadows of the buildings stretched across the street now as the sun moved closer to the tree line atop the western ridge.

Nellie clung to the hope that Willie might be found; yet at the same time she felt self-conscious walking along beside a man with such a dignified look and Sunday attire, while she was barefooted and ragged in her faded gingham. He didn't seem to mind, and he didn't treat her like a shanty ruffian.

When they got to the D & H station, Mr. Martin stopped abruptly. Nellie immediately tensed, suspecting a ruse, and she flinched as he took her arm.

"Nellie, for your brother's sake, you've got to trust me," he said, his voice grave. "When we go inside, you've got to stop acting like a beaten animal. I've got to have your trust to gain the authorities' trust. You have to understand that if Willie is caught, he will be charged with a crime against the canal and railroad company. I'm going to present myself as his guardian and take responsibility for him. Can you behave?"

Nellie nodded. "I will. Thank you, sir," she said, wanting to believe, but still afraid to trust in the kindness of this stranger. Inside, a small icy edge of her began to thaw. She walked sedately up the stairs beside him and stayed next to him as they went through the doorway and over to the office window cage.

"Pardon," he said, respectfully removing his hat. "I need your assistance in returning a runaway, a young boy, my new ward. He was seen by his sister here." Mr. Martin paused to look at Nellie.

"That's right, sir," she told the station attendant, a youngish man with a few blond whiskers on his otherwise smooth face. "Willie ran away earlier this afternoon, riding aboard the train to Carbondale. I tried to stop him, sir. Honest, I did. It's just that he's gotten this notion of going out west from reading the serials in the *Herald* . . . ." Her voice trailed off.

Jefferson took over. "The train departed here at approximately four. Could you please telegraph over and have him apprehended at the next station and returned on the first train? It shouldn't be too late."

"It may be too late," the young man said icily as he consulted his watch.

"Please, sir!" Nellie cried. "Please, you've got to get him back."

"I'll need a description. And you are aware that he has committed criminal trespass of company transport," he said coldly, his little bit of authority taking over.

"Sir," Jefferson said stonily, his already large frame seeming to overpower the tiny station room, "the boy will continue to commit criminal trespass if he is not intercepted at the next station."

The young man flushed and shifted uneasily in

his chair. "Quite right," he said, with a small cough. "We'll dispatch a message at once."

Nellie blurted out, "He's ten, but he's small and looks about eight. He's wearing overalls and a chambray shirt, and he's got a shock of yellow hair like corn silk that won't ever lie down." She stopped, the words snagged by the lump in her throat. The thought of Willie in his cut-down, made-over, baggy clothes and his unruly hair and ways brought tears to her eyes. Anxiously, she wet her lips. "He's not a bad one," she said humbly. "But . . . but he could slip away if they aren't extra watchful."

She felt a light touch on her shoulder and glanced quickly up at Jefferson Martin, this time without flinching. He smiled slightly in approval, and some of the taut worry unraveled itself from her stomach.

The young man hurriedly tapped a message on the telegraph. Nellie worried that he might not describe Willie properly, that the message might be all wrong, that Willie would never be captured. It was hard having to put trust in so many people.

"Will a reply be shortly forthcoming?" Mr. Martin asked.

The young man nodded, and then a smug look crossed his face. He tipped back in his chair and looped his thumbs through his suspender straps. "Course it will, sir. That is, unless the lad on nights stepped out for a bit of supper." Then he turned his look toward Nellie. "Did I forget to tell you folks there won't be no more coal shipments till tomorrow? Ain't no trains coming back over the mountain tonight."

Nellie felt as if a trainload of coal had just been dumped on her. No train tonight? "No tr-train," she sputtered numbly. She turned and stared up at Mr. Martin. She couldn't go anywhere till she got Willie back. And then she was struck by an even more troubling thought: Where would she and Mr. Martin spend the night?

Chapter 22

Nellie felt Jefferson's hand on her elbow. "We should be receiving a reply shortly," he said, steering her toward a bench that ran along one wall. "Rest here while we wait. There's nothing else we can do for now."

She sank down on the bench. Once she was settled, he sat down near her, but not too close.

Nellie clung anxiously to her bundle and shifted slightly so she could view him from the corner of her eyes. She was as uneasy as a horse near a moving train. It just didn't seem natural for a body to take on the troubles of two poor strangers. She tried to think what Miss Sutton's advice would be for an occasion such as this, but the teacher's voice was silent. Nellie was on her own. She decided to be forthright.

She wet her lips and pulled herself erect. "What made you take on Pa's wager, sir?"

A smile played at his lips, and it was some time before he answered. "Providence, maybe. Or foolhardiness." He shrugged, and his look became serious.

"Just suppose, Nellie Bishop, suppose I hadn't followed you into the saloon. Have you considered what fate might have befallen you?"

No—no, she hadn't. But now the thought stung her like the back of Ma's hand on her cheek. What if Mr. Martin hadn't won her? It was a sure bet that Pa would've wagered till he lost. She shuddered at the thought of the men in Reilly's, men crude as Callahan, men who would beat her worse than Ma had, men who would give no second thought to her safety or to Willie's. But why would Jefferson Martin be associating himself with the likes of them?

"Well?" he asked at length.

"You're still a no-good gambler like my pa," she mumbled, lowering her head.

"No . . . no. . . ." He sighed deeply. "If you want the truth, I'll give you the truth."

Nellie looked up again. His jaw was set in a hard line. She nodded.

"Your pa was, well, too incapacitated to play cards. You might say he auctioned you." He broke off and turned toward her. "It would take a fool not to see how pure you are. And no, I'm not a gambler."

"Are you a preacher, sir?" she asked hopefully, although she thought it unlikely.

To her surprise, he gave a low chuckle. "No, not a preacher. Only a farmer."

"Sir, it wasn't Providence, then; it was foolhardiness," she said. "Obliged all the same," she added humbly.

This time he laughed aloud. "No doubt Willie would agree. He said you were a thorny one."

Oh, Willie. How could you? "What else did Willie say about me?" she asked, pulling herself up straight and putting her nose in the air.

He grinned, his eyes dancing with amusement. "Everything. Everything a boy would think important to say about his sister."

Her heart sank. "Everything?" she said in a small voice.

"Willie said you even play the piano better than that prissy Jennie Rockwell."

"Willie said that?"

He nodded. "If it's true, maybe you could play for the Methodists."

"Oh. . ." she said thoughtfully. The idea of church was new. Ma and Pa never concerned themselves much with God. Miss Sutton's Bible reading and admonition to attend Sunday School were all she knew of such matters. Sunday School might be good for Willie. "Do you live near town, then, sir?" she asked.

Jefferson placed his hat on his knee. "Quite a distance, a half day's journey, I'd say. But we live close to a small village."

It was far from town then, far from the canal gangs,

and far from Callahan. "There's a school?" she asked, thinking of Willie.

"Yes." He smiled. "Most likely you could give piano lessons to some of the children if you wanted. My sisters would like to learn."

"You have sisters?" she asked.

"A houseful," he said. "The youngest, Dorrie, is about Willie's age."

"Willie?" She stood up at once. "Shouldn't we be hearing from Carbondale?" she asked, walking to the window cage. "Sir, how much longer for a reply . . . please, sir?"

At that moment the telegraph began to transmit, and Nellie held her breath. How mysterious the tappings seemed, but already the operator was translating the strange code into letters. Mr. Martin had come to stand behind her and was peering over her head as the letters formed words: BOY FOUND [stop] RETURN A.M. [stop].

Willie was found! Nellie dropped her bundle. "It's a miracle," she said, turning slowly to look up at Jefferson's face in the dusky light. "Sir, perhaps it was Providence after all," she said in her relief. Then she bent to retrieve her bundle.

"Youse can take your leave," the station attendant said. "I'll be closing up now."

"One moment, sir," Jefferson said, consulting his

timepiece again. "What is the scheduled arrival for the first coal shipment tomorrow? I expect the boy to be remanded into my custody without delay."

The young man blinked. "Now there'll be a certain matter of fines to be looked after before any boy is remanded to anyone other than the constable," he said, his chest seeming to swell with every word.

Nellie gasped. A fine? They couldn't get Willie unless they paid for him? What if Jefferson didn't have enough money? She looked quickly at his face, but he didn't seem alarmed.

"Of that I am aware," said Jefferson calmly. "Now, sir, may I learn what time the first train is due?"

A flush rose on the pale cheeks of the other man. "Why, first light, same as always, unless there be some delay."

Jefferson chuckled. "I'll be here at first light, then," he said and tipped his hat. "Good evening to you. Come along, Nellie. There's nothing more to be done here tonight."

Nellie walked along beside him in the warm dusk, her head spinning with questions, her bundle dangling loosely from her hand. What did he mean, "*I'll be here?*" Did he think for one moment that he could keep her away from Willie? What would he do with Willie when he got him back? He couldn't just keep him without Ma and Pa's say-so? Could he? She clutched her bundle again as she followed Jefferson down Front Street and began to wonder about her own fate.

"We're going to the hotel, where we will take supper and put up for the night . . . in separate rooms," he spoke simply. "Now, before we go to the livery, can you give me your word that you will conduct yourself decently and that you won't run away?"

"Where would I run to, sir?"

He snorted. "Where to? Where to, indeed?" He shrugged. "By now I'd guess you'd have charted out several ways of escape in that stubborn head of yours." But he didn't say it meanly, as Ma would. He spoke in the way she would speak to Willie out of fear for his safety. He said it as if he liked her thorniness. And another small part of her thawed.

Nellie nodded her head. "I give you my word, sir. I won't run away."

"I don't believe you'd give your word unless it was so, but it's also not likely you'd run off without your brother along," he said.

They had arrived back at the horse and buggy in front of Samuel Brothers. Jefferson reached over to take her arm and help her up. But Nellie pulled back and stepped up into the carriage on her own.

Chapter 23

Nellie stayed hunched in a corner of the buggy as Jefferson guided his horse along the wheel-rutted streets. Each jolt served as a reminder to her of where they were headed. What would folks say, seeing such a young girl going into a hotel with a man? But then, who would care? Ma? Pa? Her plight was of no concern to anyone other than herself.

Jefferson reined up the horse and buggy in front of the National Hotel on lower Second Street. It seemed strange to be staying so near Ma and Pa; the tumble-down shack was on the hillside just across the river. Nellie peered up at the sturdy brick of the hotel. The sign outside the establishment proclaimed fair patronage to "Commercial and professional men, jurors, and farmers." There was no mention of women or children. Hundreds, perhaps thousands, of times she had hurried past this very spot, yet never had she really seen it before. Such was her haste to get past the stablehands and other men who were often loitering about.

Jefferson alighted as a man came from the hotel's livery to attend to the horse.

"How do, Martin," the man said as Jefferson handed him the reins. "Got yourself a little passenger tonight?" The man's clothes were rumpled and soiled from stable work; he had the eyes of a drunkard. He raised his brows in question, his mouth twisting in mirth, his look suggesting to Nellie a most unwholesome mind. She was surprised to hear Mr. Martin chortle loudly and slap the man companionably on the back. She stiffened in alarm.

"What a blackguard you are," he said jovially enough. "This is Nellie Bishop, my sister's child. Ran off, wanting to get herself a look at town. Wouldn't you know, the lot fell to me to get her back." He shook his head. "Come down here, now," he said, holding out an arm toward her.

Nellie prickled at the lie and was about to blurt out a retort when her good sense grabbed her. "I'm perfectly able to get down by myself, Uncle Jeff," she said, banging her elbow on the wheel as she jumped away from Jefferson's outstretched hand. "Need you be telling every blessed soul the circumstances of my existence?"

The man's brows rose higher. "Ain't tamed, that's for durn sure." He spat a stream of tobacco juice on the ground, all sign of interest in her presence gone from his eyes. He turned his attention to the horse. "What you think, old girl?" he muttered. He clicked his tongue and started toward the livery.

"Wild and unruly as a pasture rose, you are," Jefferson said, shaking his head.

Hesitantly, Nellie touched his sleeve. "Thank you for protecting my honor," she said.

He swung around. "Your honor? I have my own honor to protect as well. But did you ever once consider that?"

She backed away, struck by the truth and coldness of his reply. No, she hadn't. She had thought only of herself. She stood on the street before the steps of the hotel and tightly clasped her bundle in both arms. She stared at him and waited. Perhaps now he would refuse to lodge her—where would she go? Confusion buzzed in her head. Wasn't freedom what she longed for?

"Come along," he said, his voice sounding troubled and tired. He didn't move toward her, didn't touch her. She walked up the steps and into the hotel behind him, her heart beating frantically with renewed fear.

Inside the door was a small front room with a long counter and a man behind it lounging on a stool. "Good evening, Martin," he said, his eyes lighting agreeably as Jefferson came forward. His expression changed to surprise at the sight of Nellie. He stood up. "And will Madam require separate lodging?" His voice held none of the scornful delight of the stable-man. Instead, it seemed to Nellie that he had asked this same question without noted interest many times before, though not to Jefferson. That was apparent.

Jefferson pulled the register toward him and dipped the pen in the bottle of ink. "A room next to mine will do, if you please," he said. He repeated the story of her running away. "Perhaps I should have custody of her room key. She might still have some foolish notion of escape."

The desk clerk nodded in sympathy and stared at her as if she were a hooligan. "Your sister will be for-ever indebted to you, sir."

"That's not likely, John," he said, with a sigh of res-ignation. "One does not often receive appreciation for acts of philanthropy, I've found."

The man inclined his head in agreement as he located the key for the extra room.

Nellie stood to the side, her face stinging and surely bright with color. She had not begged him to come to her aid. No one was forcing him to give her protection now. What exactly was he about?

"And John," Jefferson said, picking up the keys. "Send up fresh towels with soap and hot water to each of our rooms right away. We'll be taking supper in the dining room presently."

Jefferson nodded to her, and she followed him through an arched doorway, into a passage, and up a flight of dimly lit stairs.

Chapter 24

Jefferson stayed just outside the open doorway of Nellie's room until the towels and soap had been brought up. His manner remained somewhat subdued, and she wondered at the cause. Was he sorry that he had taken on this burden of two street ruffians? She couldn't blame him if he were. Still, she knew not what intentions he had for her.

"I'll come for you in a quarter hour," he said, closing the door. Nellie heard the key turn in the lock, and she was alone.

She stood just inside the door and for a moment surveyed the room. It was a nice room, carpeted, heavily draped, clean by all appearances. There was a chest, a real bed, a bowl and pitcher, and an ornately framed mirror without cracks. It was quite grand, really, and it was hers at least for the night. She dropped her bundle on a chair and cautiously pulled aside the drapery. Outside the window was the brick wall of another building. The wall was windowless, and Nellie felt secure enough to open her window and let a rush of cool evening air sweep in.

She undressed and carefully lay her clothing on the bed, smoothing out the folds of her gingham with her hands. Then she set about freshening up. She poured the water into the washbowl and picked up the delicate cake of scented soap.

She began to imagine smelling fragrant as a rose and not of harsh soap and coal and kerosene. She lathered herself slowly, enjoying the rich suds. Oh, how she would love to sink into a tub full of this sweet perfume.

As she rinsed, she was startled to catch sight of her smiling reflection in the mirror. It was a very pleasant smile, too. She touched her face in wonder.

A knock sounded on the wall behind her bed. Mr. Martin must be ready to collect her. Hurriedly she dried herself. As she fastened her frock, she thought how selfish she had been in allowing herself the enjoyment of the room when she had no idea how Willie might be faring. Would he have any food? Was he being treated like a criminal?

A thump sounded on her door. "Jefferson here." The key turned in the lock. She was surprised to see how young he looked with his face freshly scrubbed and the earlier tiredness erased. He seemed pleased at her appearance—she saw that in his eyes as he studied her face—and there was something almost boyish about him, though he didn't smile as he inclined his head in greeting. "Will you have supper with me?" he asked.

How could she refuse? Surely she was at his mercy. Still, he seemed to be giving her a choice. As if to answer for her, her stomach rumbled noisily. The only food she had eaten that day was the hunk of cheese Willie had given her.

She nodded, and together they descended the stairs. As they neared the ground floor, the clink of dishes and the sound of voices in conversation drifted up to her. She tensed. A bar of scented soap did not a lady make. She was still Nellie Bishop, barefoot and shabbily dressed. She pulled back into the shadows as they walked along the corridor.

"Remember, you are a runaway. By now, all of the hotel inhabitants are privy to this information," he whispered, leaning close to her ear.

She drew in her breath and would have stopped, but he drew her along firmly.

"Indeed, they will stare, but remember, being a runaway covers a multitude of other sins," he said, still pulling her along. "Do you understand?"

She nodded, her head hanging low. She supposed that among her "multitude of sins" were her improper attire and, perhaps, lack of social graces. But the inquisitive, entirely male population of the room stared only briefly as she and Mr. Martin were led to a table in a quiet corner of the softly lit room.

Mr. Martin ordered the spring lamb with peas for them both. How could she eat when Willie was not likely to have any food tonight? But eat she did when the meal was set before her. It had none of the tough and greasy, boiled-to-death look of the meat she was accustomed to. The meal was arranged attractively on the plate with a bit of green jelly and a sprig of fresh spearmint, and she watched Mr. Martin to see how it should be eaten as she drank from her water glass.

She ate slowly. It was so grand an evening for her, but why would he treat her so well? She had to know. She swallowed the last morsel of meat and looked across the table. "Mr. Martin, um, Jefferson, sir, I would like to know what your intentions are. What do you plan to do with me?" she asked, balling her napkin up in her hand.

He sat quietly and stared at his plate. "My first intention," he said slowly, "was to take you for my wife. And though I have been awarded that right, I'm sure it is not the appropriate or wisest course of action." He stopped and raised his head and looked directly into her eyes. "I am, in part, Delaware Indian from my mother's family, and I was taught that all people should live free and in peace. We have been called heathen and savage, but we do not sell our children, and we do not violate the chastity of any woman. And so, Nellie Bishop, I say you are free to go at any time."

He placed the key to her room on the table before her. "You are free also to stay, to come with me tomorrow, to wed me and to work with me. You are free to do as you will." Then he continued to eat as if he had not even spoken, as if he were alone.

She stared at the key in the middle of the table, and the voices around her seemed to drop away. She was aware only of her own breathing, his movements as he ate, and the key. *The key.*

Chapter 25

She was free. Free! It was true. He would let her go. Nellie put her hand on the key, still warm from his, and closed her fingers tightly around it. This was the feel of freedom! She could go to work at Samuel Brothers; she could earn her own keep; she could pay Mr. Martin back all the indebtedness she had caused him.

She glanced across at him. He was watching her. Hastily, Nellie looked away. Once again she had thought only of herself. How could she? No one had ever done so much for her. Not Ma nor Pa, not Miss Sutton, no one. Callahan would have forced himself on her, or left her on the street, or beaten her. She shuddered as his brutish face reared itself in her mind. He was a man who gave no honor to women.

"Thank you, Mr. Martin," she said in a small voice. She studied his face now. How different he seemed from Pa, from Callahan, from the men who had carted off her sisters—different even from

Willie. Yet he seemed to want something more from her than he was telling. She opened her mouth to speak, but he put up a hand to silence her.

"Nellie, do not speak hastily of your judgment of my proposal. I am too tired to talk further. You may let me know your decision in the morning."

She followed him meekly to their rooms. His only comment as he left her was "Good night."

Good night? How could she expect to sleep? She dropped down on the bed. What should she do? If only she could seek advice from someone, but whom? Miss Sutton? Willie? Miss Sutton would act righteous and lecture her on the virtues of being clean in body and soul. And Willie? She smiled as she thought of his cheerful face. Dear Willie. Willie would dream only of lawless adventure. It was impossible to stay angry at his badness, even though he had put her in a fix.

She went over to the window and leaned out on the ledge. There was nothing to see but the brick wall, darkening now as the squares of light cast from the hotel rooms were extinguished one by one. The lights from her room and Jefferson's were only a hand's width apart, and soon his went out, too.

She turned away from the window, and as she did her gaze fell upon the bundle she had dropped in the chair earlier. She carried it over to the bed, untied the knot, and smoothed open the tattered material.

She took up the rag doll, then the locket, but set them aside. When she picked up the *McGuffey Reader* given to her by the teacher, the rose she had picked from the Rockwells' bush slipped from the pages to the floor. The petals had shriveled and were already turning brown. She scooped it up and laid it in the palm of her hand. How close to Jennie Rockwell the rose had made her feel; how dear its acquisition had seemed. She started to slip the decaying flower back into the book but instead went to the window and let it drop from her fingers into the dank alley below. As it disappeared into the darkness, she felt lighter somehow, the way she thought a horse might feel at the end of a long day when it was freed of its harness and bit.

Then she tied up the bundle for good and began to ready herself for bed. What if she stayed, went to work for Samuel Brothers? Would that make her free? It was impossible to forget the way Mr. Samuel had looked at her or to forget his dark warning. And how could she walk out anywhere in the streets without fear of Callahan?

But she would be independent, paying her own way, no burden to Ma and Pa, able to help provide for Willie, and that was something.

She and Willie would be separated though. She wouldn't be able to see him often, once a week maybe, and she'd have no way to keep him away from the canal gangs any longer or to discourage his thieving ways. Still, she had come up with a plan for herself and for Willie that could work. Might work. Maybe.

Jefferson Martin had swayed her some with his talk of piano lessons and Sunday School, and with his kindness toward her and Willie. But how could she know that going with him would be a better way? Nellie covered her face with her hands. Her head throbbed from trying to sort it all out. She couldn't. Not now, not in one night.

When she had stripped to her undershift, she turned down the light, took the key in her hand, and climbed into bed. How soft the mattress was! How quickly her eyes drooped with a will of their own. She fought with the sleep that was drugging her body. Tomorrow's reckoning was so near, and she had not yet clearly resolved what she wanted. Still, as she drifted into sleep and her fingers holding the key loosened, something quieted within her.

Chapter 26

Nellie awakened with a jolt from a dream. She sat up in bed at once, her heart thudding slow and hard against her ribs like a blacksmith's mallet striking down against an anvil. It was dark still, so black that she could barely see anything in the room other than the movement of the cool night air troubling the drapery.

She trembled, her bare arms prickling. It all seemed clearer now. She had to get Willie away from town. In some strange way Willie had been right. They needed to get away, not just from Ma and Pa, but from town. In the end, it was this town that would rob Willie of his dreams.

She climbed out of bed and began to dress quickly. She must not let that happen. If only daylight would come and she could go to Jefferson, give him the key. He would take it. He had told her she had the night to decide, and now she realized that she did not want him to go, for she was beginning to think of him as a friend—maybe her only friend. She pulled the chair over next to the door and sat waiting for morning. She wanted to be ready when he came for her.

As the first gray fingers of dawn seeped into the room and she heard him outside in the corridor, she threw open the door. He blinked in surprise, and before he could utter a word, she thrust the key into his hand. But he didn't seem to catch on to its implications. He just stood there, facing her, waiting, it seemed, for her to speak. She lost all courage to say the words. Her hands grew clammy and her throat constricted. She lowered her lashes and bit her lip instead. She had thought that giving him the key would be answer enough.

"Willie," she whispered, raising her head. "Willie!" she said now with urgency in her voice.

"We'd better hurry to the station," Jefferson said. He swung away from her, and there was nothing to say or do except hasten after his quickly receding back.

Apparently he had left word, although how and when he had done so she had no knowledge, because when they emerged from the hotel, his horse and buggy were standing by the steps for their departure. She was little aware of anything in the early morning mist. She stationed herself on the edge of the seat as though to hurry them along on their mission. Jefferson, his movements quite hurried, seemed as intent as she, although he remained outwardly calm.

It surprised her, though, when they arrived at the station and he did not immediately leap to action. He took his time with hitching up to a nearby post, so much so that she began to wring her hands and pace up and down on the boardwalk alongside the buggy.

"The train's not in. It's a ways off, by the sound," he said, stepping up on the walk.

She stopped. Yes. She could hear it now, far away and not too clear. Why hadn't she noticed it before, and she the one waiting for her brother? She studied his face. He *was* different, she thought slowly. He noticed things, things other people might miss. Again a pang of something went through her, and she thought how nice it would be if she could be that way. Instantly she stopped fussing and waited for his direction.

"It would be wise to settle with the clerk quickly before Willie's arrival?" He posed this as a question, and seeing that he expected her to decide, she nodded.

"Y-yes," she said. It wasn't usual for a man to give up the right to have all the say.

"I suppose," he said, as he began walking toward the station, "I suppose your brother will have fared just fine."

"How so?" she asked indignantly, pulling away in surprise. Then she blurted out, "But there is such wickedness!" Her voice dropped, and she shivered with remembrance of her encounters with Callahan. "Wickedness and horrible doings, but how could you know that? You couldn't know what the canal rowdies are like. You couldn't know how fearsome they are," she said hotly.

"I've met a few just recently," he said slowly, drawing out his words.

"Oh." She could feel her face flame. Of course he had—her pa was one.

"You underestimate your brother. He's winsome and clever in his own way. A good-natured lad like him can get through a lot of rough spots easy enough," he said as they walked up the steps and into the station.

The morning clerk was much older and more heavily built, with a white halo of thinning hair circling his head. He was busy writing in a ledger of some sort, but he stopped his work and looked up as they approached.

Jefferson related in a steady voice the events of the day before. Nellie took quiet notice that he said nothing of the younger man who threatened to get the constable.

The older man broke suddenly into a laugh. "Lads these days, always one or two got to find a little adventure." He stopped and squinched up his eyes. "I might have done that once upon a time myself. Not saying I did, course; not saying I didn't, neither." He winked at them. "Now and then a person has to look the other way. Now mind you, I'm not saying that's what I'm gonna do, but if you'd like to strike a deal, I might just be busy when the train comes in."

Studying the man's face, Nellie wasn't sure what he meant. He seemed of two minds, and this unsettled her.

She looked to Jefferson for an answer and was startled to see that his sun-darkened face had grown deeply red and his eyes held an anger she had not seen before. When he spoke, it was with the same steadiness of earlier. "It would be best to uphold the rules. I am quite prepared to pay the proper fine for the lad's release."

The man wanted the money for himself! That was what he meant by all that waffling. How foolish she was for not guessing. Nellie looked back at Jefferson and then down at her feet. She would have been willing to pay the lesser amount and be done with it, and then worried if it had been the right thing later on, or worry that the constable might still come one day with papers for prosecuting. She was abashed at this revelation of her own streak of dishonesty.

There was tense silence as Jefferson locked eyes with the other man. All at once, the station attendant waved an arm and shrugged as if nothing had transpired. "As you wish," he said, shoving a paper under the grate. "Sign where it says on the line, and pay what it says on the bottom." Jefferson cupped the upper part of the page to hide it from Nellie's view as he wrote out his name.

She was about to ask if she could read it but was interrupted by the train whistle. She clasped her hands together and watched through the window for some sign of Willie. "Willie!" she cried out, as she saw him being escorted along the track bed by an attendant.

He was grinning, his face lit the way it would be when he had seized an especially fine treasure. He waved and called out "Nellie!" —then started toward the door. But he was held back by the man accompanying him.

Her stomach twisted into knots as she feared that somehow Willie would still be carted off, but soon he came into the station and Jefferson strode forward with the paper. Willie ran toward her, and the ordeal was over at last. She actually hugged him, a thing she had never done, and found that her face was wet with tears.

But where was Jefferson? She turned around, and there he was, standing by the doorway, his hat in his hand. Pulling Willie by the hand, she walked across the station floor.

Her palms turned sweaty again, and her heart raced, but this time she breathed deeply and swallowed back her fear. "Please don't leave," she said—but they weren't the right words. She swallowed and tried again. "I'd like to go with you."

"Nellie Bishop," he said her name slowly. "Well then—we'd better head home."

Home. That was what she had longed for.

Willie broke in upon their exchange. "You're not leaving me behind. I'm going, too, ain't I?"

Nellie drew in a quick breath and looked at Jefferson. "He must!"

"He has to," Jefferson said, waving the paper. "This document makes me responsible for keeping him out of trouble. I have arranged for your folks to be made aware of this action."

There was much to talk about as they left the station and rode up Front Street. Willie seemed quite beside himself. "It's just like the ending of a western serial in *The Herald*," he said.

Jefferson shook his head and gave a hearty laugh as he urged the horse onward.

Nellie smiled at her brother's fanciful notions. But she was content to sit quietly by as they drove through the town. When the houses finally disappeared from sight, she sank back weakly against the cushions as the relief of leaving swept over her. She didn't know what the future would hold—but in this one moment, she felt unburdened and free.

Afterword

My great-grandparents, Daniel Jefferson Martin and Nellie Almira Bishop were united in holy wedlock on August 31, 1886, at Hancock, New York. Nellie was fourteen years old. They were the parents of seven children, the first-born being my grandmother, Clara Martin Keesler, mother of Naomi Keesler (Annie Lucas of *Annie's Choice*).

My great-grandfather, Daniel Jefferson Martin, was half Indian. He died of pneumonia in 1906 and was buried in Wayne County, Pennsylvania, in Lake Como Cemetery. My great-grandmother died at the age of ninety-one in 1963. She is buried in Dyberry Cemetery in Wayne County, Pennsylvania. I remember her well and loved her dearly—she had a keen wit and a matriarchal presence that commanded both awe and respect.

Other characters in the book are drawn from stories and memories related to me by my great aunt, Dora Martin Welsh.

—*Clara Gillow Clark*